Forget Me Not

A Novel by

TERRY BUSH

Plus a bonus short story:
One Dark Night

ISBN: 979-8-89079-017-0 (Paperback)
ISBN: 979-8-89079-018-7 (Ebook)

"If you prick us, do we not bleed? If you tickle us, do we not laugh? If you poison us, do we not die? If you wrong us, should we not revenge?"

—William Shakespeare

Kerry

Thanks for making a long trip enjoyable.

This book is dedicated to Patricia Mary Bernadette James and the memory of my amazing parents, Kathleen and Leslie.

You are a lovely lady and will find happiness

Best

Tom

Table of Contents

Also By
The Author

Crescent Street – 2017
The Passion and the Madness – 2020

Acknowledgment

I'd like to acknowledge and thank Chris O'Byrne for his assistance in arranging the publication of this book.

Prologue

Some are born into unfortunate circumstances, while others are born with privilege. But no person knows their final destiny until the journey through life reaches its conclusion.

Chapter One

Hatfield, England – May 1960

When fifth-form high school student Roger Williamson woke up on Saturday morning, he felt a sense of purpose and optimism that had previously eluded him.

Facial deformities and bodily injuries, the outcome of parental neglect during his infancy, had, unfortunately, left him as a physical oddity. Additionally, standing barely four-feet-seven-inches tall, he was by far the shortest boy in his year—an outcome, most probably though not certainly, of his mother spending a night with a circus dwarf in exchange for a bottle of gin and five shillings. These combined attributions had made his school days a seemingly never-ending series of ridicule, isolation, and occasional bullying.

But despite his tragic past, the last few days' events had given Roger reason to believe his future may be taking a turn for the better. While walking home from school earlier in the week, he'd struck up a conversation with a classmate, Diane Coleman, a quiet-spoken, modest individual, though inwardly mature and insightful

1

for her years. As a result, she recognized Roger's daily challenges and was one of the very few people who treated him like a normal human being. She also knew that Roger, like most boys his age, was attracted to the fairer sex though his disfigurements had resulted in most girls avoiding him. To ease this burden, Diane occasionally used tongue-in-cheek humor. "So, tell me, Roger, which lucky girl is getting your attention nowadays?" she asked lightheartedly.

Roger felt himself blushing though he knew this could be difficult for others to notice as much of his face was a mottled reddish-purple color. When he regained his composure, he playfully retorted, "I thought you knew by now that I only have eyes for you, Diane."

"If only I could be so fortunate," Diane smiled sweetly. "But seriously, who's top of your list at the moment?"

Despite his embarrassment at the topic being discussed, Roger felt more comfortable talking with Diane than with any other person he knew. "Well, I suppose Margaret Carpenter comes to mind," he said, chuckling. "But I doubt she even knows I exist. And even if she did, she'd probably run a mile."

Standing five-foot-nine-inches tall, with long shapely legs, a full bosom, thick blonde hair, and pale blue eyes, Margaret, a fifth-form C-stream student, was considered the most attractive girl at Trinity High School. While Diane had no personal interaction with Margaret, she was aware of the attention many boys gave her.

Diane hadn't given her conversation with Roger any further thought until the subject was indirectly raised during a playground discussion that included a boy from the B stream, John Webster. While talking with a group of students about plans for the weekend, John mentioned that he'd be going to the youth club Saturday evening dance with his elder sister and her friend Margaret Carpenter. Thinking on her feet, Diane took John aside when the group broke up. She cautiously asked, "John, you said that your sister is a friend of Margaret Carpenter. Are you also one of Margaret's friends?"

"I'm not sure I'd call her a friend, but we are on talking terms. Why do you ask?" John said, displaying apparent interest in the individual being discussed. Following a moment of hesitation, Diane said, "It's a rather delicate matter, so can I rely on you to keep this conversation strictly between us?"

Intrigued by Diane's question, John responded, "Of course, mum's the word."

"Well, it concerns a classmate of mine, Roger Williamson."

At the mere mention of Roger's name, Diane saw John's face take on a look of disdain. "You mean the boy with the—you know," he said, touching his cheek with his forefinger.

"Yes, facial scars, the result of severe burns suffered when he was just two years old," Diane said contritely, annoyed by the obvious ignorance being displayed. However, this was not the first time she'd experienced similar reactions. Diane silently questioned the wisdom of proceeding with the conversation, finally rationalizing that while she had nothing to lose, she may have something to gain.

"Roger is a very good person. He's also astute. However, given the painful scars he carries with him that were not his making, he's had to deal with the contempt of many stupid and biased people," she said, emphasizing the word stupid.

Diane paused for a moment and, in truth, was rather enjoying that John had gone red in the face though it hadn't been her real purpose to embarrass him.

"Like most boys, Roger is attracted to girls. While many students are not mature enough to see past superficial physical issues they find unattractive, I'm certain that you don't have such childish traits, and that's why I'm seeking your help."

Diane's switch from mocking criticism to flattery quickly accomplished the outcome she'd hoped for.

John stood straight, and a smile of self-satisfaction spread across his face. "How can I help you then?" he asked, unwittingly imitating his vicar's tone when addressing the Sunday congregation.

"You mentioned your relationship with Margaret Carpenter. As I'm sure you're aware, she is widely considered one of if not the most attractive girl in our school."

Though Diane had not sought a response to her statement, the expression on Roger's face provided clear evidence of his concurrence. She continued, "If Roger were to meet with Margaret and word of that meeting were spread around, it would undoubtedly improve his standing with many students, which, in turn, would almost certainly make him much happier."

"So, what do you want me to do?" John asked, still trying to figure out where the conversation was leading.

"I'd like you to arrange a meeting between Roger and Margaret outside school hours. And, of course, explain to Margaret the real purpose of such a get-together. If she's a decent person, I can't see any reason she'd refuse such a request, as, after all, it's no skin off her nose."

John stopped to think. Given Margaret's popularity, he wanted to avoid saying anything he might regret later. But he privately knew Margaret to be an utterly selfish individual who expected everyone to treat her as if she were royalty. And while she was currently friends with his sister, he thought this was probably a temporary relationship, likely resulting from his sibling's infatuation with being seen in the company of a widely admired female. "I'm not sure that she'll agree to such a meeting," John finally said, with the self-confidence he'd previously shown draining from his face.

"Why on God's earth not?" Diane said, a little louder than she had intended.

"Look, Diane, I'll be frank with you. I'm almost certain that Margaret wants nothing to do with Roger. Between you and me, she's not the sort of person who'd willingly help anyone, especially if there's nothing in it for her."

Diane restrained herself from verbalizing her inner reaction to John's commentary, but when her blood pressure returned to normal, she said softly, "John, I appreciate your honesty. And I recognize that we can only try our best. However, I would really appreciate you asking Margaret, and we'll just have to accept whatever her response is."

The only words John could muster before running to his next class were, "Okay, Diane, I'll see what I can do. But I'm not making any promises, as I think it's improbable Margaret will agree."

When the bell rang to signal the end of the school day, Diane accepted that her proposed plan had no realistic chance of succeeding. Though usually not one to give up easily, she reluctantly agreed with the need to drop the idea rather than continue fretting over something doomed for failure.

On Thursday, Diane skipped lunch and spent an hour in the library, revising her history notes to prepare for the upcoming O-level exams. While packing her papers and getting ready to attend the two o'clock geography lesson, John Webster suddenly appeared at her side with a wide grin.

"Diane, you won't believe this. Last evening on my way home, I bumped into Bob Lane. You may know him. He's a classmate of mine, a tall boy with wavy brown hair. It occurred to me that Bob is closer to Margaret than I am, so I told him about our conversation."

At first, Diane was irritated, as John had agreed that their discussion on the subject was to be kept private. But given the circumstances, she calmly waited for him to continue.

"Bob spoke with Margaret during morning break, and guess what? She agreed to meet with Roger this coming Saturday. I'm unsure of the place or time, but I'll find out this evening and let you know first thing tomorrow."

Diane's face lit up, and she did something totally out of character. She threw her arms around John's shoulders and kissed him full on the lips.

Diane set off for school earlier than usual on Friday morning, and when she reached the main entrance, she patiently waited for John to arrive. When he did, she rushed to his side, bubbling over with anticipation. "Did you get word from Bob?" she blurted out.

"I most certainly did," John said. "Tell Roger that Bob will wait for him on the corner of Station Road and Blackthorn Street at ten o'clock tomorrow morning. From there, he'll take Roger to meet Margaret."

"Thanks, John. I can't tell you how much I appreciate it," Diane said, immediately rushing to inform Roger of the arrangements.

Excited at the potential of what lay ahead, when Roger jumped out of bed early on Saturday morning, he headed straight for the bathroom. The previous evening, he'd ironed his Sunday-best trousers and checked to ensure a fresh white shirt was in his wardrobe. He'd also polished his black leather shoes. When fully dressed, he performed a final check, examining his appearance in the large mirror on the hallway wall. Satisfied that he looked presentable, he proceeded into the kitchen where his Aunt Dolly was brewing tea.

"My word, you're up early this morning, young man. It's only seven-thirty. Did you remember it's Saturday, so there's no school today?" she said, turning away sharply to hide the surprise of seeing her nephew wearing his finest clothes.

Roger was too embarrassed to disclose the real reason for his appearance, and while he had no wish to tell untruths to the woman he adored, he felt that a white lie was excusable considering the circumstances. "There's a meeting at the school this morning to discuss preparations for the upcoming O-level exams. So, I wanted to look my best." He said, desperately hoping his aunt would believe him and not pursue the subject in more detail.

Dorothy (Dolly) Williamson was the elder sister of Roger's mother, Elizabeth Williamson. A midwife and committed spinster, Dolly had taken Roger and his mother into her care many years prior when it had become apparent that Elizabeth could no longer look after herself, let alone her two-year-old son. While her intuition told her that Roger wasn't giving a complete account of his agenda for the morning, she knew him to be a responsible young man. Consequently, she chose not to question him further on the matter. To Roger's relief, Aunt Dolly smiled and said, "What time do you have to be there?"

"Nine-thirty," Roger said, allowing himself leeway for his ten o'clock rendezvous.

"Then you have plenty of time for a wholesome breakfast. I'll make you scrambled eggs, bacon, and toast. That should fortify you until you get home. Speaking of which, what time can I expect you back?" Aunt Dolly said.

"Not exactly sure, Aunty, but I'm guessing around one o'clock."

"Okay, hopefully, your mother will be up by then," Dolly said woefully, knowing that her sister had been extremely intoxicated the previous evening, which had long since been a regular event. Roger gave his aunt a knowing look though he refrained from commenting.

Following a hearty breakfast, Roger revisited the hallway mirror for a final inspection. Upon satisfying himself that his appearance was still in order, he kissed his aunt and set off for his appointment with Bob Lane.

Roger arrived at the intersection of Blackthorn Road and Station Street fifteen minutes early, his excitement and anticipation at an all-time high. But when Bob Lane hadn't shown up thirty minutes later, Roger thought the whole episode had been a hoax.

Concluding that he'd simply been on a fool's mission and feeling thoroughly dejected, Roger had just started his journey home when he heard a voice calling out his name behind him. On turning around, he saw Bob running towards him. "Sorry I'm a bit late; I got held up unexpectedly," Bob said without further explanation. "Just follow me. Where we're going is only a five-minute walk."

The two boys walked halfway down Station Street before turning into a cul-de-sac ringed with red brick-terraced homes. When they reached the house at the far end of the circle, Bob asked Roger to wait while he went inside. Moments later, he reappeared, beckoning Roger to join him. Sauntering across the room on his tiptoes, Bob led them through the hallway, stopping at the living room door. There, he looked towards Roger while placing a forefinger onto his lips before quietly opening the door, surveying the room, and finally gesturing for Roger to enter.

Once inside, Roger's first sight of Margaret was her rear profile as she stared out the window, admiring the flowers growing in the back garden. She wore a white blouse, a navy-blue skirt that stopped several inches above her knees, and black high heel shoes.

"Hello, Margaret," Roger said excitedly, beside himself being alone with the best-looking girl he'd ever known, "Thank you for meeting with me."

On hearing Roger's voice, Margaret turned around abruptly, causing her long blonde hair to swirl around her shoulders. When she caught sight of Roger, her facial expression froze; then she put her hands to her mouth while screaming, "What are you doing here, you fucking freak? Get out of my sight immediately, you horrible little creature, before I make your face even uglier than it already is—if that's even possible!"

After Margaret's verbal tirade, Bob Lane and his friend, Paul Jeffries, burst into the room, laughing hysterically at the performance in front of them.

Numbed by what had just happened, when Roger regained control of himself, he ran outside the house, tears streaming from his eyes. With Roger's departure, Margaret turned toward the two boys, still laughing at her. "If you thought that was funny, you are very much mistaken!" she yelled. "It's about time you acted your age. And as for you, Bob Lane, don't you ever speak to me again!" After which, she stomped out of the house, slamming the front door behind her.

"How did you set that up?" Paul asked when Margaret left, still chuckling at the spectacle he'd witnessed.

"The opportunity came about by accident," Bob said. "I've meant to get one over on Margaret for quite a while. She's a snotty bitch, and we've had a love-hate relationship since the second form. I know she's currently sweet on Kevin Shaw, the captain of our boys' club football team. So, I told her I could arrange a meeting with him at my house today because both my parents would be out at work."

Roger took the long way back from Bob Lane's home, trying to regain his composure though tears of embarrassment and anger still flowed down his cheeks. He'd been subjected to teasing many times in the past, and he'd been physically pushed around occasionally. Once, he'd even been spat on. But never, ever, had he suffered the humiliation he'd endured during those few moments in Bob Lane's living room. Fortunately, by the time he reached home, he'd managed to get his emotions under control. And with more clarity of mind, he made an impromptu decision. Despite knowing that missing his O-level exams would change the career path he'd previously had in mind, he swore that he'd never, ever step foot inside Trinity High School again. Undoubtedly, his aunt would try to persuade him against this action, but whatever the consequences, his mind was firmly made up.

Chapter Two

<u>Milan, Italy – 1990</u>

At nine o'clock Friday morning, Antonio Esposito leaned back in his brown leather chair, looking expectantly at the gold-plated telephone perched on his mahogany desk. He was hoping to receive a phone call any minute that, if positive, would signal the beginning of the next chapter in his extraordinary life. Moments later, his secretary's head popped through a small opening in his office door, "I have Switzerland on your private line, sir," Maria Bruno said, vanishing as quickly as she'd appeared. Antonio sat on the edge of his chair and took a deep breath as he picked up his phone. "It arrived this morning, Mister Esposito. I'm happy to inform you that it's already been cleared. Please accept my congratulations," the voice on the other end said.

On receiving confirmation that 90,000,000 US dollars had been deposited into his anonymous Swiss account, Antonio lit a Havana cigar and inhaled deeply. Then he watched the plume of smoke he'd just exhaled slowly make its way up to the cut-glass chandelier hanging from the vaulted ceiling. With the blood gushing through his veins at the thought of what the future might hold, Antonio strolled across his office and opened the sliding door that led onto a private balcony. Once outside, he took a deep breath while slowly scanning the piazza six floors below, lined on all sides with restaurants, outdoor seating, and retail outlets. As usual, various people were milling about, some in formal attire hurrying about their business, while others, mostly casually dressed, were relaxing over coffee or window shopping. While taking in the scenery, Antonio reflected on the unimaginable success he'd enjoyed since starting his business in Milan eighteen years prior. And while he would miss the city's excitement, he was keen to get started on the plans he'd drawn up for his future.

With his mind still racing, Antonio returned to his desk and stubbed out his cigar before picking up his phone and summoning his secretary.

"What can I do for you, sir?" Maria said on her arrival.

"Take a seat, please, Maria. I have some news that likely will come as a surprise to you. I've just sold my business, so I'll be moving on immediately. I don't know if the new owner has a position for you or if you want to continue working here when I'm gone. If you are interested, call this number on Monday morning." Antonio said, handing over a red and green business card. "I want you to know, however, I've been very pleased with your work these last seven years, and I offer you my sincere thanks and best wishes for the future."

Though trying hard not to show it, Maria was devastated by Antonio's news, especially as she and her family relied heavily on her income. "I'm not sure if I understand, sir," she mumbled, trying to hide the tears slowly filling her eyes. "I thought the company was doing well?" A question that she didn't expect would be answered.

"All good things must end, my dear," Antonio said without elaborating.

Maria doubted her boss's sincerity, and resentment filled her mind, feeling she was casually tossed aside, much like a used paper handkerchief. But her mood quickly changed when Antonio reached into his desk drawer and handed her a check in an amount that exceeded the accumulative salary she'd earned since being in his employ. "Why, thank you so much, sir. That's very generous of you," she said, suddenly feeling guilty by her initial reaction.

"You're very welcome. I'll be taking off in an hour, and you can do likewise though there are a couple of things I want you to take care of before you leave."

"It would be my pleasure, sir."

"Make a noon reservation for two at Angelino's. Then call Dickson. Tell him to meet me there for lunch; he must collect my wife and take her to Genoa afterward." The final directive caused Maria to involuntarily raise her eyebrows, a reaction Antonio immediately picked up on. "Oh, perhaps I forgot to tell you," he said with a smile, "I got married recently."

Maria's expression slowly changed to a knowing look, as in all the years she'd worked for Mister Esposito, he'd never stopped surprising her.

Chapter Three

Dickson, a nickname that Antonio Esposito gave Ricardo Ferrante at their first meeting, was the youngest of four brothers raised in a small village on the outskirts of Palermo in Sicily. Ricardo's mother, Sofia, spent most of her time attending to household needs though when needed, she assisted with gardening duties in the family smallholding. At Ricardo's birth, his father, Matteo, was a rising star in the local mafia. Upon leaving school at age thirteen, Matteo started as an errand boy for the organization, following an introduction from a classmate. Despite beginning on the bottom rung, Matteo quickly rose through the ranks, having quickly demonstrated his devotion, skills, and unquestionable loyalty, which always got the mob's attention.

In his elevated role, Matteo involved his sons in the business when each of them turned twelve. He believed this would enhance his career and lay the foundation for a lucrative future for all his family members.

Ricardo often listened to his father relaying stories about the mafia during infancy. However, the implications of these tales hadn't registered with him until he was eight. When they did, they shocked him to the core. But despite his trepidation, he suppressed such feelings, as his instincts told him that revealing them would not be well received by his father. However, as the months passed, Ricardo realized the day would come when he would be required to participate in such activities though he tried his best to put the matter out of his mind. But inevitably, one summer day, shortly after celebrating his twelfth birthday, he was summoned to a meeting with his father and his eldest brother, Lorenzo.

When they were all seated on the back patio, Matteo said, "Ricardo, you are no longer a boy; you are now a young man. This coming Saturday, you will accompany Lorenzo on the first step of your new career. Your task will be simple; it only involves helping collect money from a farmer who hasn't paid his bills. Lorenzo will tell you more about that when the time comes. Make me proud, young man," Matteo said, kissing his son on the forehead before disappearing into the house.

Early Saturday morning, Ricardo and Lorenzo set off on foot to a local pig farm. "What do you want me to do when we get there?" Ricardo asked during their journey, his voice shaking with dread at what the response might be.

Lorenzo pulled a six-inch blade from his inside coat pocket, "Just showing the farmer this," he said, "is probably all it will take for him to hand over the money. But if that doesn't work, I'll ask you to grab his daughter and threaten to cut her throat." With that, Lorenzo pulled out another blade and handed it to Ricardo.

Fortunately, the farmer cooperated when Lorenzo exposed his knife, feebly complaining, "This is daylight robbery; what do I get in return?"

"Protection is what you get," Lorenzo answered with a sneer.

"Protection from what?" the farmer said meekly.

"The first time you fail to pay up, you'll find out." Lorenzo said coldly, telling Ricardo, "Let's go, little brother. We're done here for the time being."

Ricardo was still shaking when he went to bed that evening, and while he hated what was happening to him, he knew this was now his lot in life.

Following his first exposure to the mafia and their modus operandi, Ricardo's involvement in the family business gradually increased. At age thirteen, he had his first experience of threatening someone with a knife. At age fourteen, he helped break a crooked drug dealer's leg. At age fifteen, he knocked out several teeth from a non-complying customer while his brother held the man in a headlock. At age sixteen, he stabbed a woman in the thigh after she'd disobeyed his father. And at age seventeen, he fatally shot a man who had obtained information potentially damaging to his family and the mafia. Ironically, while he'd grown to hate himself and his work, this last act brought him sufficient acclaim from within the clan. As a result, he was promoted and put in charge of the local prostitution ring the following year.

Ricardo's responsibilities in his new role initially appeared straightforward, even though he was disgusted at the immorality of the business he found himself in.

He had four brothels assigned for him to manage, each located in low-density areas on the city's perimeter. Every establishment had several resident bodies for rent and a security guard who protected the assets while discouraging the occupants from attempting to escape. The latter was primarily carried out by verbal abuse or threats, but they would inflict physical punishment when deemed necessary. However, in such an event, it was important that the guard not leave any visible evidence that might make the victim undesirable to potential future customers.

While Ricardo's marching orders included the necessary financial results, there was little guidance on how they should be achieved. He was required to produce a minimum monthly profit of $5,000, from which he would personally receive ten percent. If he failed to pay this amount, he wouldn't receive any payment though he would get back-pay compensation if he made it up during the following twelve months. Furthermore, if the annual target of $60,000 was not met, his position would be reviewed. While being reviewed had no specific objectivity, Ricardo was aware of how the mob typically dealt with the performance they determined to be inadequate. As an additional incentive, however, Ricardo was promised that if he ran the business to the clan's satisfaction for one full year, he would be given more territory and, therefore, the opportunity to make additional money for himself.

Fortunately, Ricardo met the financial criteria required of him, and true to their word, one year later, the clan fulfilled their promise after having acquired a suitable premise in the neighboring town of Messina as a starting point for potential future growth. To get the business off the ground, Ricardo hired a temporary deputy to help oversee the Palermo business, allowing him time to focus on the new location, which, if successful, would be the hub for further expansion. Ricardo's first duties were to arrange the necessary security while discreetly promoting the new business. When this was accomplished, the mob would supply the girls. This was primarily achieved through their human trafficking network, wherein they'd find vulnerable candidates and feed them with drugs until they became addicted. Once addicted, most girls would readily agree to provide services for an ongoing supply of drugs, food, shelter, clothes, and a little pocket money.

Given all he'd learned during the previous year, Ricardo was confident he'd handle the expansion program without undue problems. While this was the case, it wasn't long before an unexpected challenge arose. Though the mob's typical recruiting came via their trafficking program, one girl had been acquired from an orphanage. Her name was Greta, a pretty sixteen-year-old with large, dark-brown eyes.

Ricardo had long since learned that it was always wise to keep interaction with his girls to an absolute minimum, as any hint of a personal relationship or favoritism could quickly lead to unwanted circumstances. Consequently, he knew very little about any of the females under his management other than that they were largely desensitized and often unpredictable. But from the beginning, he sensed something different about Greta though he initially could not identify precisely what that *something* was. However, he got his first insight when one evening, after escorting two of his girls to a popular pick-up point, he returned to find Greta lying face down on her bed, sobbing uncontrollably. Finding one of his girls crying was not unusual for Ricardo, but there was something about Greta's distress that was different. The sound she was making didn't relay the simple anger he'd often heard from the other girls; instead, it was a message of hopelessness. Ricardo's first reaction was to ignore the matter, but against his better judgement, his sense of empathy guided him in a different direction. He placed one hand on Greta's shoulder and asked softly, "What's upsetting you, young lady?"

Moments later, Greta rolled over and, through swollen eyes, said, "I miss my mother terribly. And even worse, I don't know where she is or if she's still alive."

"What happened to her?" Ricardo asked, intently listening while Greta told her story.

Greta Mancini, the only child of Vincent and Giovanna Mancini, was born and raised in a rural area thirty miles southeast of Palermo. Their home was a small stone cottage on two acres of fertile land, which had been inherited by her father, having been in his family for three generations. To earn a living, Vincent repaired shoes and various household items, while Giovanna grew fruit and vegetables, selling the excess to local families in the area. While their occupations only produced a modest income, they satisfied their prime goal in life—to maintain self-sufficiency.

Shortly after Greta celebrated her eleventh birthday, a red Mercedes pulled up outside the family home when she and her mother were drinking coffee on the front patio early one morning in the springtime. A tall, suntanned man dressed in a black suit got out of the car and walked over to her father, who was adding the finishing touches to a lawn mower he'd been repairing. "Are you Vincent Mancini?" The man asked bluntly. Her father, a gentle God-fearing soul, was taken aback by the brusque nature of the man's question, as such an aggressive interaction was unusual in the neighborhood. But when he regained his poise, Vincent replied politely, "Yes, I am. How can I help you, sir?"

The man said that he would deliver a white Fiat sedan at sunset the following day. Immediately upon its arrival, he wanted the bodywork painted green and the tire rimes painted white. Furthermore, all the work needed to be completed in time for the vehicle to be collected the day after delivery.

Vincent was wary of the situation he unwittingly found himself in, as he suspected something untoward was taking place. But not having an aggressive nature, he tried to finesse his way around the issue. He respectfully told the man that he couldn't complete that amount of work in the required time frame, assuming that would end the matter. Vincent, however, hadn't reckoned with the type of person standing in front of him. "Don't give me that line of bullshit, old man," he said, pulling a wad of used bank notes from his jacket pocket and casually tossing them at Vincent's feet. "This is for your trouble, so as you can see, I'm not asking for any favors. Just do as I say, and all will be well."

Vincent tried to clear his mind as he found himself caught in a dilemma. While his instincts told him that he shouldn't involve himself in something that sounded so inappropriate, he also knew his family could put the money to good use, especially as they hoped to send their daughter to a private school when she turned thirteen. Eventually, he rationalized he wasn't doing anything wrong by taking on new business, so reluctantly, he bent down and picked up the money.

Before departing, the man stared at Vincent and said through clenched teeth, "Don't you dare let me down, Mancini. And make sure that neither you nor any member of your family says a word about this to anyone—not now, not ever." As if to reinforce his statement, he opened his jacket to reveal a revolver tucked into a shoulder holster. "We wouldn't want anyone to get hurt now, would we?" he said, pointing at his gun before climbing back into his car and driving off at high speed.

When the Mercedes disappeared, Greta's parents sat down to discuss what had just taken place, and as with most family issues, Greta, since turning ten, was allowed to listen in. Her parents agreed that the matter was, at best, highly suspicious and that it would be preferable if it could be avoided. The problem now was, how could they possibly explain that, having accepted the money, they'd chosen not to carry out the work? And to add to their quandary, there'd most likely be severe and possibly dangerous repercussions in such an event.

Having discussed the pros and cons, Vincent finally decided that it would be okay for him to carry out the work, his rationale being, "I can honestly say that I wasn't aware of assisting any act that was immoral or illegal." Though in his heart, he knew he wasn't telling the whole truth by making such a statement.

No member of the Mancini family slept well that night, and they all prayed that the man in the black suit would turn up and simply ask for his money back. But their prayers were not answered. Shortly after sunrise the next day, the same red Mercedes pulled up outside their cottage, only now with a white Fiat in tow.

Upon seeing the cars arrive, Vincent Mancini ran out to meet the man in the black suit. "Take these," the man said, tossing a set of keys to Vincent while the driver of the Fiat climbed into the Mercedes passenger seat. "Make sure the work is finished by sunset tomorrow. And don't forget, not a word to anyone." He shouted through the window of his Mercedes as he accelerated away.

"The following morning, my father reluctantly began working on the white Fiat," Greta said. "But two hours later, he felt uncomfortable with his decision, so he stopped work to discuss his feelings with my mother. He told her that he was now certain he was doing something improper, and because of that, God would not approve of his actions. My mother agreed, so they both took off for our local church to seek guidance. The priest told them that my father needed to 'take the appropriate action,' informing the police exactly what had happened. He pointed out that it was for law enforcement to investigate if they felt it appropriate and not an issue that my father should make judgements on."

"What happened then?" Ricardo inquired.

"That evening, the man who'd delivered the white Fiat came to collect it, and after satisfying himself that the job had been done to his satisfaction, he drove off without saying a word. Naturally, we all prayed that was the last we'd hear of the matter. But unfortunately, it wasn't. The police tracked down the Fiat and, in turn, located the two men who'd used it as a getaway vehicle for a bank robbery. Unbeknown to us, the police officer in charge of the case had given instructions for one of his deputies to visit our home and advise our family on appropriate measures to be taken in the event of anyone connected to the crime visiting us with bad intentions.

But they didn't act quickly enough. Within hours of the arrest, the man in the black suit arrived at our home, only this time, he was driving a maroon BMW. It was around six o'clock, and our family had just sat down for dinner. The man didn't bother knocking on our front door; he just barged in. Once inside, he lifted my father from his chair and pushed him against the wall. He took a knife from his belt and slashed it twice across my father's throat in a split second. With blood gushing down his shirt, my father's body slowly slid down the wall, finally slumping onto the floor.

Despite my naivety, I undoubtedly knew my father was dead. While this happened, my mother let out the most piercing scream I'd ever heard, and then she fainted. Freaked out by the horror I'd just witnessed, I willed myself to attack the man. I picked up a brass candlestick holder, intending to hit him over the head. But he quickly overpowered me, and then he took me outside and locked me in the trunk of his car."

"You poor thing," Ricardo said, "What happened next?"

"I was driven off at high speed for what seemed like an eternity. All the while, my mind kept reliving the horror of what had happened, and frankly, I just wanted to die. Eventually, the car stopped, and the man who'd captured me opened the trunk and tried to lift me out. Again, I attempted to hit him, but he grabbed my arm and slapped my face so hard that I realized resisting was pointless. With no viable options, I surrendered, leaving my future to fate."

"Where did the man take you?" Ricardo asked.

"To an orphanage located in a deserted area three miles outside Agrigento. The facility housed approximately forty children, whose ages ranged from three to sixteen years. The women in charge of the facility were quite strict, but life was bearable if you followed the rules.

The man in the black suit who took me there came back to visit occasionally. On each occasion, he told me I'd be released when I grew up and that he had arranged a lucrative future for me. At the time, I wasn't sure what his definition of grown-up was, though it eventually became apparent that he was referring to these." she said, cupping her ample breasts in her hands.

"Two weeks before my sixteenth birthday, the man in the black suit came to collect me. While he didn't provide details of where we were going or what he had in store for me, I must admit that I'd rather gotten my hopes up. But they were soon to be dashed. He took me to a house used as a mafia training facility, where I was to be indoctrinated into my new profession. That was the most humiliating and degrading experience I think a girl could be subjected to. I'd prefer not to go into detail, but let me just say that it included losing my virginity in an undignified and crude manner and, of course, against my will."

Ricardo waited for Greta to regain her composure because it was clear that reliving this memory brought great mental anguish. When she collected herself, she added, "Shortly after my 'job training,' I was delivered here to work under your control."

Listening to Greta's story brought about a strong sense of guilt and remorse for Ricardo, something he hadn't experienced when dealing mainly at arm's length with the other girls in his charge. He wanted to hug Greta and tell her how sorry he was for what she'd experienced, but he knew that he'd been warned about such feelings and the unwanted results that could arise should he ever act on them. Notwithstanding, he kissed Greta lightly on her forehead and wished her well before taking off to check on his other girls.

Her story frequently crossed his mind in the days following Ricardo's chance encounter with Greta. He assumed this memory would gradually fade, but as days turned into weeks, the opposite happened, and he found himself developing an increasing urge to learn more about Greta. Trying hard to rationalize his feelings, Ricardo wrestled with the possible explanations, as one of them didn't match the person he considered himself to be. He surely couldn't be falling for a prostitute. Granted, Greta was attractive though so were most of his girls. But at the same time, why was he judging Greta without looking in the mirror? After all, he was a pimp, so for him to point out the immorality of a girl working under his control was nothing short of blatant hypocrisy. Finally, he decided there was only one answer, which was to create an opportunity to spend time alone with Greta to establish if he was really interested in her or just experiencing an irrational or unexplainable fantasy.

Chapter Four

Saturdays typically involved half the girls working inside the brothel, while wealthier clients collected the other half and returned them the following morning. By late afternoon, business was well underway, and Greta had been told she would be picked up at seven o'clock to spend the night with a client. When the cab arrived, it took Greta to a hotel on the city's south side, where the receptionist directed her to a luxury suite on the rooftop level. Upon opening the door to the designated room, Greta was suprised to find Ricardo waiting there for her. She assumed his presence could only be to allow him to introduce her client for the evening, so she was confused when he offered her a seat before politely saying, "Greta, first, I want to apologize for having you sent here under false pretenses. There isn't a client waiting for you; I made this arrangement solely to create an opportunity to spend time alone with you."

Angered by the deception that was taking place and frustrated by her inability to influence the outcome of the situation she found herself in, Greta said through clenched teeth, "There's no need to sugarcoat your objective. What you want from me is clear, so let's go into the bedroom and get on with it."

Realizing that he'd failed to start the discussion in the direction he'd hoped and recognizing that Greta had, perhaps understandably, misinterpreted his intention, Ricardo took a deep breath, trying desperately to find the words and the tone he was looking for.

"Greta, I understand why you responded the way you did. It was my fault for not fully explaining why I had you brought here this evening. All I ask of you is to listen to me for a few minutes. If you want to leave, I'll arrange a cab to take you back. And I give you my word that if that's what you choose to do, I will never hold it against you. Does that seem fair?" Ricardo finally said, desperately hoping he'd managed to lower the tension and set the meeting in a better direction.

Greta was caught off guard by Ricardo's response. Since the day her father had been murdered, she'd trusted no one even vaguely connected to the mafia, regardless of their actions or their words. And though Ricardo had treated her compassionately when he'd found her distraught on her bed, she'd assumed there had to be an ulterior motive. Eventually, she said, "Look, I don't know what you want from me other than to turn tricks for your financial benefit. But if, as you say, you want me to listen to you, then I suppose I have no options."

Ricardo thought the situation was hopeless and that he might as well give up on his endeavor. Nevertheless, given that he had Greta alone and could see no downside to telling her truthfully why he'd arranged this situation, he continued.

"I know it must be hard for you to believe what I'm about to say, especially given our respective roles in the prostitution business. But believe me, Greta, like you, I hate what I do every day, and also, like you, I don't do it out of choice. I was born into a mafia family, and what I do today was expected of me from the time I was born. After I found you crying several weeks ago, which led to you telling me your story, it stirred many thoughts in my mind that I suppose I'd simply suppressed or tried to ignore over the years. At first, I didn't see the connection, but gradually, I realized that although it seems somewhat ridiculous on the surface, we're in similar situations."

Ricardo remained silent for a while, and Greta thought she saw a sad look on his face.

"Besides that realization, I sensed you were a sensitive and caring young lady and, quite possibly, someone I'd like to befriend if circumstances were different. Over the last few weeks, I've thought about you a lot and paid more attention to you each time I see you. That being said, because of our respective roles and the presence of the other girls, I've never been able to talk with you in the way I'd like. So, in a nutshell, I arranged for us to meet this evening, hoping that we could learn more about each other."

Ricardo clasped his hands together and looked towards the heavens before continuing.

"I think I've now told you everything that was on my mind, so as I said earlier, we can talk more if you wish, but if you prefer not to, I'll call a cab to take you home. And again, whatever you decide, I promise not to hold it against you in the future."

Greta stared at Ricardo, unsure of what to say or do. While Ricardo had appeared to be sincere with his words, she couldn't help but think he might be setting a trap for her though she could not come up with an idea of what that might entail. Finally, thinking there was little downside to seeing where Ricardo wanted to take things, she said, "Okay, let's try to learn more about each other. But can I be sure that if things get uncomfortable for me, we can end the evening and that your promise will still hold?"

"You have my word," Ricardo said, smiling for the first time since Greta had arrived.

When Ricardo woke on Sunday morning, he found Greta's head resting gently on his shoulder, with her slow, rhythmic breaths flowing across his chest. While enjoying the warmth permeating from her partially naked body, he knew he needed to get her back to the brothel to avoid unnecessary speculation regarding her overnight whereabouts. On the drive back, Ricardo relived the events of the previous evening. It had started awkwardly, and for a moment or two, it looked like it could end abruptly and embarrassingly. Fortunately, Greta's conciliatory remarks provided a platform for further discussion though he never imagined where it would lead. Over several hours, they touched on a myriad of subjects, agreeing wholeheartedly on most issues while respectfully disagreeing on others. And as the evening advanced, the chemistry between them gelled.

But notwithstanding the satisfaction Ricardo was getting from the way the evening was progressing, never in a million years would he have anticipated Greta's final words, "When I first caught sight of you earlier this evening, Ricardo, I immediately assumed you had me sent here simply for us to have sex. And as we both know, if that is what you had wanted from me, I would have had no choice. But throughout this evening, I realized my judgement of you was incorrect.

"Consequently, I apologize for my attitude earlier. It's getting late, so we need to decide where I will spend the night. I should leave if you want to send me back to my living quarters. On the other hand, if, as you've suggested, we try to build on the relationship we've started this evening and see where it takes us, then perhaps it would be appropriate for us to spend the night together. By that, I mean just to snuggle up in bed, as I don't think it would be helpful for us to make love until and unless it feels like the right thing for both of us."

In the days following his night with Greta, Ricardo was preoccupied with conflicting thoughts. While he'd always loathed the role he'd inadvertently found himself in, he'd been able to focus on the job at hand. But now things were totally out of kilter. And to make matters worse, his current mindset would likely harm his job performance, which could bring about grave ramifications for himself and his family.

Deciding he needed time alone, he summoned a local street gang member to deputize for him while he took a few days off to think the matter through. The individual he contacted went by the name Blood, a tall, muscular teenager who Ricardo would not have fancied his chances against if it ever came down to a fight. Fortunately, this was not an issue, as Blood knew only too well the consequences of messing with the mafia. Finding his older brothers' severed arm inside a sack on his doorstep one morning following an unauthorized drug deal was a lesson he'd never forget.

"I'll be back in three or four days, and I expect everything to be in good order when I return." Ricardo said bluntly, "And by the way, Blood, I'm sure you'll enjoy your evenings with the merchandise while I'm gone. But take a tip from me; avoid the dark-haired girl who goes by the name Greta. She has a sexual disease with no cure, and I've heard it can be painful and deadly."

Knowing that a change of scenery would help him relax and improve his mindset, Ricardo cast his mind back to places he'd visited in the past. In doing so, a distant memory brought a smile to his face. It was an incident on a family camping vacation during which his father had spent one whole day fishing with no success. Frustrated by this failure, his father eventually stomped off, cursing under his breath and abandoning his fishing tackle. Being a curious young boy, Ricardo cast his father's line back into the water. He immediately felt the pole being pulled from his hands.

And given that he was only six years old and fearing he'd be in trouble if he lost his father's equipment, he immediately shouted for help. Moments later, his father reappeared, and after taking control of the situation, he reeled in a four-pound snapper. Later that evening, while cooking dinner at the campfire, his mother, much to his father's embarrassment, gave Ricardo a hero's welcome, saying, "My son, you single-handedly saved the whole family from starvation!"

This memory inspired Ricardo to throw the essentials for a short trip into a backpack. Then he took off on the one-hour drive to the village of L'Aquino, stopping only briefly at the spot where the legendary fish had been landed nearly twenty years prior. Upon arrival, he checked into a small family-owned boarding house renowned for its outstanding food and hospitality.

Three days and two nights of walking along the Oreto riverbank and dining on local cuisine gave Ricardo the ideal environment to contemplate his future. But though he now knew beyond a doubt that he wanted a new direction and purpose in his life, he couldn't devise a practical plan, especially knowing that you didn't just quit the mafia if you valued your existence. He realized, to get out of his current situation, he'd have to effectively disappear and find a new home, but the problem was—where could he possibly go? He knew another part of Sicily wasn't a viable option, as the mafia would surely find him.

It had to be another country, but which one? And how would he survive when he arrived? And then there was the question of Greta. He'd like to take her with him wherever he went. But would she be willing to go with him? And what sort of future could he offer to her, anyway? There were just too many unanswered questions. He realized he needed to seek sound advice from someone he could trust completely. But who could he go to for that? Only one possibility came to mind—and even that may present yet another set of issues—nevertheless, Ricardo eventually decided it was worth a try.

Armed with the knowledge that his father and his brothers would be at work in the city center, Ricardo visited his mother on a Tuesday morning. "Oh, what a wonderful surprise. It's so lovely to see you, Ricardo." She said when answering a knock on her front door. "Would you like some coffee or tea?"

"Coffee, please, but could we sit on the back porch?" Ricardo said, for though he knew they were alone, he felt a stronger sense of privacy when sitting in the garden.

"Yes, of course. Why don't you make yourself comfortable, and I'll bring the coffee as soon as it's percolated?"

Ricardo was still reviewing the speech he'd rehearsed when his mother appeared. "Here you go, my darling." She said, placing a coffee pot, two large mugs, and several croissants on the table. "It's always lovely to see you, Ricardo, and as you know, I like surprise visits. Though I feel there's a particular reason for your coming here today." She said, raising her eyebrows slightly.

Ricardo took a deep breath and was about to embark on the speech he'd tried to memorize when his mother interrupted. "I can tell something is troubling you, dear. Just relax and take your time. Then when you're good and ready, let me know what's on your mind." She said, taking hold of Ricardo's hand.

He was quickly put at ease, something his mother had always done, so Ricardo verbalized his situation and uncertainties in the same uninhibited fashion he'd done as a youngster. And as he was sure she would, his mother listened carefully without interrupting until he'd finally said his piece.

"First, Ricardo, I want you to know that I completely understand your feelings and desires. However, as I'm certain you are aware, our family must deal with several complex issues, some of which we have little or no control over. As your mother, naturally, I want the best for you, but I also must consider how the actions of one family member might impact another. So, I'd like a little time to think things over. Why don't you visit again in two weeks? Hopefully, that will give me enough time to ponder the possibilities."

Each evening, Ricardo ticked a day off from his calendar. His mother was an exact woman, so when she'd said, "Visit with me again in two weeks," he knew she meant precisely that. Consequently, it did not surprise Ricardo that when he knocked on the front door of his family home at ten o'clock on the allotted Tuesday morning, his mother promptly opened it, kissed him, and led him to the back patio where hot coffee and croissants were waiting.

Chapter Five

Bianca Ferrante, formally Bianca Barone, was born and raised in a farming community in southern Sicily. Her father was a horse groom at the local stables, and her mother took in the laundry while keeping house and raising her two daughters. Both her parents were devout Catholics, so Bianca spent much of her early years attending church services, and at age nine, she began participating in their social and volunteer events.

Through these pursuits, she was involved in various activities, which were occasionally attended by a boy named Matteo from a nearby village. Given that he was three years her senior, blessed with swarthy good looks, bright blue eyes, and a muscular frame, he received the attention of many young females, leaving Bianca as just another one of his long-distance admirers. But shortly after she celebrated her thirteenth birthday, an unexpected event took place, which Bianca referred to later as divine intervention.

A small church group had spent a Saturday afternoon visiting elderly citizens in the village, aiding with household chores that were becoming too difficult for the occupants to carry out by themselves. Bianca was making her way home from her final house call when Matteo, who'd also been involved in the event, suddenly appeared at her side. The two of them struck up a conversation, which led to Matteo inviting Bianca to join him on a hike through the countryside the following weekend, and from that moment onward, the couple were inseparable. Shortly following Bianca's fifteenth birthday, Matteo asked for Bianca's hand in marriage. Though her parents had reservations, they finally bowed to their daughter's wishes, enabling the couple to tie the knot six months later.

Understandably, Bianca did not know that her husband was already involved with the local mafia, as she believed him to be a truck driver who delivered goods and collected the corresponding payments. But when the nature of Matteo's real job surfaced, she prayed for guidance, as she now had a six-month-old son to consider and was already pregnant again.

She felt uncomfortable discussing her dilemma with her parents, so Bianca confided in her cousin Liza. The two of them were of similar age, and they'd enjoyed a special relationship since being toddlers, even though their time together had often been interrupted by rifts between their respective families. But notwithstanding these obstacles, Bianca and Liza had always shared their fears, ambitions, and most intimate issues, comfortable in the certainty that their words would never be divulged to another party.

"Would you like cream in your coffee, Ricardo?" his mother asked when both were seated on the back patio.

"Yes, please, mother. I'd also like a large spoonful of sugar in mine." Ricardo asked coyly, as his mother had always preached the damage this substance could cause to one's health.

"I've done a lot of thinking since we last met," Bianca said while passing a mug of coffee to her son and politely ignoring his request for sugar. "As I told you when we last met, I must care equally for every family member. This, of course, sometimes presents difficulties when the interests or desires of one individual conflict with another." Bianca stopped to look her son square in the eyes and was encouraged to see his head nodding. "Naturally, I don't wish to upset any family member in finding an appropriate solution to another member's issues. But occasionally, and I believe this to be the case in the current circumstances, it's unavoidable."

Bianca took a sip of her coffee, but surreptitiously, she wanted to allow her son to comment. When it became clear that Ricardo had decided to remain silent, she continued, "As you may or may not know, I've always been very close to my cousin, your Aunty Liza. I've now had the opportunity to discuss your situation with her, and as it turns out, she may be able to help. But before I proceed with this, I want to ensure you're comfortable keeping her involvement strictly confidential?"

"I have no problem agreeing to that, Mama. But purely out of interest, why do we rarely see her if you've always been close with Aunt Liza?"

"That's a rather delicate subject that I'd prefer not to discuss at this moment, but let me just say that the virtues her family holds don't always mix well with those on our side of the family."

Ricardo's mind was awash with thoughts as it slowly dawned on him how much his mother had likely sacrificed to keep her extended family as close together as possible. He would have liked to express his gratitude, but the appropriate words eluded him.

"For reasons I've already touched on, it's also been a long time since you've seen your cousin, Alberto, Aunty Liza's son," Bianca said.

"Wasn't he at Grandma's funeral?" Ricardo asked, causing Bianca to look skyward and cross her chest before saying in a whisper. "Yes, he was." And following a moment of reflection, Bianca continued, "Alberto showed an interest in design during his school days. And because his father was doing well in the import/ export business, he could send Alberto to a prestigious university to study architecture. After his graduation, Alberto secured a job in Milan, where he now resides though he still visits his parents regularly. I met with him when I visited my cousin last weekend. Alberto came up with a possible solution for your current state of affairs. But before taking it any further, both he and I need to know if it's a potential opportunity you'd be interested in pursuing."

"Believe me, Mother; I'm prepared to do almost anything to get out of my current situation and be free to live the life of my choosing."

"You realize that any move you make carries its risks," Bianca said, hoping her son knew what these might entail without further explanation.

"I know the mafia believes there is only a way in but no way out. Naturally, I need to evaluate the possibility that Alberto has in mind, but assuming it provides a reasonable chance for me to escape, I'm willing to take it. Frankly, I'm more concerned about the risk to Greta than myself." Ricardo said with a forlorn look.

Bianca was surprised by her son's final remark. He had told her on his previous visit that he'd formed a relationship with one girl under his charge, but she'd not understood his intention to take her with him if he were to escape from his current predicament. This became more complicated because Greta, though most probably an innocent girl cursed by unfortunate circumstances, was, nevertheless, a whore.

Ricardo picked up on his mother's reaction and the likely reason for it. "Mother, I know Greta is in a line of work that offends your morals. I understand that, but it's not her fault. If you were to meet her, I'm sure you'd see what a kind and considerate person she is."

While her son's words did little to change Bianca's concern, she remembered her naivety when she'd fallen in love with Matteo. And while she hoped and prayed that Ricardo would not live to regret following his emotions, she decided that given the circumstances, the right thing for her to do was support him. "Very well. I'll visit with Liza this weekend, as Alberto will be home then. Hopefully, he'll be able to meet with his contact in Milan and get more specific information on the possibilities. I'll call you as soon as I have an update."

Ricardo waited patiently to hear from his mother, during which time he spent many hours pondering over whether to inform Greta of the escape he was contemplating. Initially, he'd assumed she'd accompany him if a viable option became available. But on reflection, he realized he might be misjudging her wishes. Furthermore, until there was a concrete offer on the table, what was the point of raising Greta's hopes if, ultimately, they could be dashed?

Finally, Ricardo got word from his mother, and the following day, he set off to the family home. And as he could have predicted, his mother awaited his arrival, and she'd already brewed the coffee.

"My dear Ricardo, I sincerely hope I'm not jumping the gun, but I have some encouraging news to share with you," she said with a radiant smile.

"I can't wait to hear it," Ricardo responded excitedly.

Bianca described her meeting with Liza and Alberto; the latter just arrived for a weekend visit. Alberto had confirmed that he'd met with a wealthy businessman with whom he'd been acquainted earlier in his career. He'd explained Ricardo's circumstances and the escape opportunity he sought. Alberto had been hoping that the businessman would know someone who'd be able to facilitate such an arrangement. Still, to his surprise, he was told, "Actually, I may need the type of person you're describing though, of course, it would be subject to agreeing on terms."

On hearing this news, Ricardo jumped up from his chair and hugged his mother tightly. "Thank you so much, Mother. You've always come through for me. I just don't know how to thank you enough!"

Bianca smiled lovingly at her youngest son, "I appreciate your kind words, but I've done very little. It's Alberto you need to be thanking. And just a word of caution, it's not a done deal. I believe strict conditions will be attached to any offer, so assuming you get one, you still need to be certain the terms are acceptable."

"Mother, I think it's improbable that I'll find any terms or conditions unacceptable if the opportunity enables me to escape my current circumstances and be free."

Though Bianca shared in her son's joy, she couldn't help but wonder what conditions a wealthy businessman might want to impose on a young man he'd never met, especially one he knew to be a member of the Sicilian mafia. She was also curious why Ricardo hadn't mentioned Greta, but she wasn't going to open Pandora's box.

"Given that your response is obviously yes, the next step is for you to visit Milan and meet with Alberto's contact. If you take the early morning ferry from Messina, Alberto can arrange a car for you when you arrive in Reggio. Then you can drive yourself to Milan. I doubt the meeting will take long, so you should be able to get there and back in only two full days. That way, you can avoid explaining an extended absence if anyone is curious about your whereabouts."

Ricardo didn't need further explanation. He had long been aware that his mother could handle family issues while considering the workings of the mafia. He only hoped and prayed that he'd have the same wisdom his dear mother possessed one day.

The following Thursday, having visited his Aunt and cousin Alberto to thank them for making the arrangements, Ricardo rose at dawn and set off to Messina. On his arrival, he caught the first ferry to Reggio, where the car Alberto had arranged was waiting for him.

From there, he immediately hit the road to make his six o'clock dinner appointment with Mister Antonio Esposito at Angelino's restaurant in Milan.

Despite dealing with the frustration of several traffic jams, Ricardo arrived at his destination with twenty minutes to spare. He used the time to freshen up. Having made himself as presentable as possible, he made his way to the dining room entrance where the maître d', a stout baldheaded man dressed in a black dinner suit, was waiting to greet the guests. "Can I help you?" he asked brusquely, looking Ricardo up and down.

"My name is Ricardo Ferrante, and I'm meeting Mister Esposito for dinner at six o'clock," Ricardo said, glancing at his watch to ensure he was on time.

At the mere mention of Mister Esposito's name, the maître d's tone changed, "Well, good evening, sir. Please, follow me. Mister Esposito is waiting for you in his usual spot."

When Ricardo arrived at the corner table where Mister Esposito was seated, he introduced himself and expressed his gratitude for the opportunity. "Welcome to Milan, young man. Take a seat." Mister Esposito replied, gesturing to the chair opposite him. "You've had a long journey, so first, let's order nourishment and refreshments, and then we can get down to business."

Ricardo was pleasantly surprised at the reception, as he was expecting a person of Mister Esposito's wealth to have a forceful and intimidating personality, much like senior members of the mob he'd dealt with. But while Mister Esposito appeared to be cut from a different cloth, Ricardo did not doubt that he was a man who expected to get his way.

The two men made light conversation, touching mainly on Ricardo's background and interests, that is, until Antonio washed down his last forkful of seafood risotto with the drops of Soave remaining in his glass. Then, after having wiped his mouth with his napkin, he placed his elbows on the table and rested his chin in his hands before saying in a more formal tone, "Alberto told me you're looking for a new start in life, effectively to be a new person with a new identity. There's no need for you to explain why, for while I don't know much about your current situation, I know enough to understand your desire. For me to offer you a job, there are two non-negotiable terms I need your absolute agreement to.

"First, and perhaps most importantly, there is a personal matter I need you to take care of. I don't know the exact timing of this requirement as it depends on other events, but my current guess is that it will be in a couple of years. Given your background, this requirement should be in keeping with matters you're familiar with, and as it's some way off, you'll have ample time to plan its execution.

"Second, leading up to the time of my first requirement, I would like you to assume the role of my "Man Friday." Possibly you're unfamiliar with that character, but I can describe him to you in a few short words. It's someone who will do whatever I need, whenever I need, and carry things out quickly without asking questions. Now, if we move forward with such an arrangement, compensation would be that I will provide you with suitable living quarters, a car, and a weekly allowance of 150 US dollars. This should allow you to maintain a reasonable standard of living, but the real payoff depends on completing the personal matter I mentioned earlier. When I receive confirmation that it has been completed to my satisfaction, I'll give you a lump-sum bonus of 100,000 US dollars."

Mister Esposito's statement caused Ricardo's mind to swirl. He hadn't expected an offer of this magnitude, and while he would like further clarification of what was explicitly required of him, he didn't want to blow his chances by seeming hesitant.

Antonio refilled his wine glass and took another sip of Soave, thereby allowing Ricardo a few moments to consider his offer.

"So, do we have an agreement or not?" Mister Esposito asked firmly after swallowing his second sip of wine.

"I have a couple of questions," Ricardo said, treading carefully.

"Go ahead."

"I understand the general idea of what your personal task entails. But it would be helpful to get a little more detail."

"Very well," Mister Esposito said, opening the briefcase tucked under his chair and removing a sheet of paper on which three photographs were stapled, and below them was a nine-letter word written in red ink.

"Am I making myself clear now?" Mister Esposito asked after allowing Ricardo a few moments to process the message.

"Perfectly clear," Ricardo said.

"So, what's your second question?"

"That I be allowed to bring a young lady with me."

"I have no problem with that, providing her presence does not interfere in any way with your duties and responsibilities," Mister Esposito said firmly.

"In that case, we have a deal, Mister Esposito. I fully understand what's required of me, and I give you my word that I will not let you down." Ricardo said solemnly.

"Good. I assume you need to return home to settle your affairs, so I'll expect you back here two weeks from today, ready to start work immediately," Mister Esposito said, offering his hand.

"I'll be here," Ricardo said, taking Mister Ricardo's hand and shaking it firmly.

"Well, run along then, and when you get back, I want you to come directly to my office. You said that you were looking for a new identity. Part of that starts immediately. From now on, I'll be addressing you as Dickson." Mister Esposito said.

Chapter Six

The only time Ben Hollingsworth forgot to set his alarm clock was, as he told the guests at his *wedding reception, the luckiest mistake he'd ever made.*

Benjamin Leonard Hollingsworth was born in St. Albans Hospital on June 5, 1919, the only child of Bill and Daisy Hollingsworth. Bill worked as a foreman carpenter, and before the birth of their son, Daisy was a charwoman.

Young Ben showed signs of being a bright individual from the very beginning. So, it did not surprise his parents when he proved to be an outstanding student and excelled on the football field. These achievements made his dad incredibly proud, believing his son would one day aspire to a professional career in architecture or quantity surveying. This outcome would break the family mold, given that five consecutive generations of Hollingsworth males had all worked in the building trades. But alas, Bill's hopes for his son were not to be fulfilled; while Ben was more than capable of achieving the goals envisaged for him, he chose to follow in the footsteps of the man he idolized instead.

Consequently, in September 1935, having completed the fifth form at grammar school, Ben Hollingsworth signed up for a five-year carpentry apprenticeship.

Ben's skills grew quickly, and in less than two years, he was assigned to a construction site where he would work under the direction of the lead carpenter. The project consisted of twenty new housing units in Hatfield, a town approximately six miles from Ben's home.

Being well disciplined and understanding the importance of punctuality, Ben prepared himself appropriately. The weekend before his new assignment started, he rode his bicycle to the project site, noting that the journey took precisely twenty-nine minutes. To this, he added a ten percent factor for possible adverse weather, and an additional ten minutes as a cushion, concluding that if he left home at 6:42 each morning, he would certainly get to work on time, irrespective of unforeseen circumstances. On Monday morning, Ben's careful planning produced the desired result, as without rushing, he could check in with the lead carpenter at 7:15, fifteen minutes before the official start of the workday.

"So, you're Master Hollingsworth," Bob Haskins said gruffly. The lead carpenter was well acquainted with Ben's father and held him in high esteem, but notwithstanding, tradition required that he not show favoritism due to family connections.

"Follow me, and I'll take you around the facilities. Then you can get to work." Bob Haskins said firmly, striding off with Ben at his heels.

Ben was taken to the wood machinery and storage yard after being shown the locker room, the toilet facilities, and the area set aside for lunch and tea breaks. There, he was shown the work required to prepare rough-cut lumber, which initially would be his primary task. This entailed removing or treating knots, sanding jagged edges, and de-nailing used wood surplus or timber salvaged from demolition work. At the end of the short briefing, Bob said, "Right, now get on with it, and I'll be back to check on your progress in an hour or two."

While Ben found site work physically taxing, he also found it a learning process in terms of developing skills and understanding teamwork. He paid particular attention to the latter, as his dad had explained the importance of effective relationships if he rose to the ranks of supervision or management. His dad had also made him aware of a custom that had long been practiced in the industry, "Look, Ben, you need to be aware that apprentices are nearly always a target for practical jokes. If this happens to you, don't get upset or angry; just take it in stride. Remember, this is only intended to be a test of your character. In the long run, handling it with maturity will gain you the respect of your fellow tradesmen and, eventually, the management."

Within three months of starting work, Ben had established himself as a conscientious, reliable, and courteous young man who showed talent beyond his years. Though, of course, getting to this point required Ben to handle several trials and tribulations that included finding his bicycle saddle removed and replaced with an old paint tin, discovering rusty nails in his lunch box, and ascertaining, on one occasion, that the clock in the storage yard had been set back by one hour—something that only became apparent when he realized that all the other workers had left for the day.

Notwithstanding the difficulties along the way, it came as no surprise to Ben that his dad's wisdom proved to be spot on.

Ben's stint on the Hatfield project was entering its final month when one Tuesday evening, upon arriving home from work, his mother said, "Sit down, love. I received troubling news earlier today that I need to share with you. Your grandmother had a heart attack yesterday. Your father and I are visiting Southampton tomorrow morning to visit her in the hospital. It's serious, but when I spoke to your grandfather, he was optimistic that she'd pull through. Your father is taking the rest of the week off but must be back on Sunday, ready for work next Monday. There's bread, vegetables, and tinned soup in the larder. You can pick up anything else you need from the local shops. Don't worry about the laundry; I'll deal with that when I get back. Oh, and don't forget to bring the milk in each morning. If you run into any problems, you can always call on Aunt Angela. I'll let her know what's happening, so I'm sure she will help if necessary."

"I'm sorry to hear about Grandma. Please give her my love. I'm sure she'll recover, and hopefully, we can all visit with her when she does. But don't worry about me, Mum, just take good care of Grandma. I can look after myself."

"I know you can, Ben." Mrs. Hollingsworth told her son before kissing him gently on his forehead.

Typically, Ben restricted his social life to weekends, but with his parents away, he invited his pal, John, to join him for dinner on Wednesday evening. Ben's experience with cooking was limited, but he put together a decent meal consisting of tinned soup, cheese and tomato sandwiches, accompanied by two cups of hot Oxo, all of which he and John devoured in minutes. After clearing away the dishes, Ben set up the chessboard, and the two boys embarked on a challenging match that ended in a stalemate. After the game, Ben made two more cups of Oxo, which they drank while discussing football, their jobs, and *girls*—a subject that had been increasingly on their minds recently and one that provided opportunities for much playful exaggeration.

"Good Lord," Ben said, glancing at the cuckoo clock on the parlor room wall. "I didn't realize the time. I don't mean to kick you out, John, but it's past bedtime, and I need to hit the hay."

"Likewise. Thanks for a fun evening, and I'll see you at the youth club on Saturday evening," John said as he took off on his short walk home.

Unlike his mother, Ben had never had trouble sleeping soundly, so he was surprised when he awoke before the alarm clock went off on Friday morning. Peering through glazed eyes, he was relieved to see that the large hand was on the quarter hour, giving him close to thirty minutes to prepare for his daily commute— until he looked more closely and saw that it was 7:15 a.m., not 6:15 a.m. Annoyed at himself for forgetting to set the alarm, Ben leaped out of bed, threw on his clothes, and jumped onto his bicycle, but despite pedaling as furiously as his legs would allow, he still arrived seventeen minutes late.

Knowing Ben to be a dedicated individual who always put in a full day's work, the foreman carpenter accepted Ben's apology. While this gave Ben a degree of relief, he was, nevertheless, disappointed at spoiling his perfect time-keeping record. And to make matters worse, it reignited the taunts he'd previously endured, and upon his arrival at the shed where the men took their morning tea, he was greeted with an array of caustic comments, implying that young Ben had not yet mastered the art of telling time.

With tea break over, it dawned on Ben that not only had he missed breakfast, but he'd also forgotten to pack his lunch. Though realizing that he may be putting himself in line for even more ridicule, he reluctantly asked Bob Haskins if he knew of anywhere close by where he could purchase something to eat during the lunch break.

Having witnessed the ribbing Ben had already taken, Bob went easy on his young apprentice. "Yes, a place next to the train station sells sandwiches at a reasonable price. It's about a mile from here, so you should be able to get there and back in ten minutes. But kindly ensure you're not late for the second time in one day." The foreman told Ben, raising his eyebrows.

At noon sharp, Ben took off on his bicycle and was relieved when he arrived at the station café in less than five minutes. He skimmed the menu chalked on the entrance wall before joining the line of people waiting to be served. As the line shortened, Ben got a side view of the young lady working at the counter when she suddenly glanced in his direction. For a moment, their eyes met, and the young woman smiled sweetly before turning her attention back to her work. But for Ben, the moment did not disappear quickly, as he was still mesmerized when a minute later, she asked politely, "What can I get for you today, sir?"

"I'd like a cheese sandwich on brown bread, please," Ben eventually said in a muffled whisper, realizing that his mouth had been open since they'd first made eye contact.

Every Saturday during soccer season was special for Ben, as his work finished at noon, allowing him ample time to eat lunch, change his clothes, and get to the playing field for the three o'clock kick-off. But instead of waking with his usual enthusiasm, he stared at the wall while reflecting on the previous day. It hadn't started well, as he'd tarnished his time-keeping record though that wasn't the subject foremost on his mind. Instead, the young woman who'd served him at the café occupied his thoughts. *What was it about her,* he asked himself, *that had left me speechless and embarrassed?*

She wasn't the most beautiful girl he'd ever seen, and the emotions he was experiencing were not coming from anything obvious, like the crush he'd had on Alice, which was largely attributable to her long, shiny black hair, or Jane, whose hourglass figure had aroused his physical desires. *So, what was it then?* he asked himself again. He couldn't answer the question, as nothing particular about her appearance could explain his feelings. He didn't think it could be her hair, as he'd never been especially attracted to a redhead before, nor did he care much for curls. And freckles? *Pretty unlikely*, he thought.

Furthermore, it wasn't as if they'd had a meaningful conversation—far from it. She'd simply asked for his order, and he'd only uttered, "Cheese sandwich on brown bread, please." Try as he might, Ben could make no sense of his situation, so using the logic that guided most of his life, he decided to put the subject out of his mind once and for all and get on with his day.

Following a hard-fought game against a rival youth team from the neighboring town of Hertford, which ended in a 2-2 draw, Ben and his friend, John, agreed to meet at six o'clock for a pint in the White Swan before spending the balance of the evening at the community hall where the weekly dance night was held.

"Good game today," John said while ordering two pints of brown and mild. "You played well, Ben, but you looked a little distracted. Am I right?"

"Unfortunately, you are," Ben replied without explaining.

"Okay, are we playing games? Or are you going to spit out what's bugging you?" John said.

"It's a silly thing, really, and it makes little sense," Ben said, staring vacantly into his beer.

"Okay, enough of the drama. Will we have a proper conversation, or will you continue behaving like an old woman's blouse? If you are, I might just as well spend the evening alone," John said.

John's words resonated with Ben, who quickly realized his demeanor was inappropriate for an evening out with his friend. "I'm sorry, John. I didn't mean to be a party pooper. Look, I know this sounds ridiculous, but I briefly met a girl yesterday, and for some reason, I just can't get her out of my mind."

"In that case, I'm guessing she had big tits," John said with a cheeky grin spreading across his face.

While his friend's response did not amuse Ben, he knew he was only trying to keep the mood light. "You may be surprised to know that I didn't notice," he said.

"Pull the other one; it's got bells on it," John said playfully.

"I'm being serious, which makes it even more difficult to explain how I'm feeling. She was working behind the counter and wearing a white smock, so I only really saw her face." Ben said, still trying to rationalize his infatuation with a girl he'd only set eyes on for a few moments.

"So, what about her got you so turned on?" John asked nonchalantly. And without waiting for an answer, he added, "Anyway, drink up, and let's go dancing. Maybe you'll find another face to fall in love with tonight." He said, mocking his friend lightheartedly.

Chapter Seven

When Ben woke up on Sunday morning, he suffered from a mild hangover. Usually, he restricted himself to two pints of beer on a Saturday night, but in an endeavor to brighten his mood, he'd consumed twice that amount. Trying to liven himself up, Ben jumped out of bed, washed his face with cold water, then tucked into three slices of toast, which he washed down with a mug of steaming tea.

Knowing his father would return from his visit to Southampton later that evening, he tidied up the house while deciding how to spend the rest of his day off. Thinking a bike ride to Rickmansworth would help him relax, he prepared lemon curd sandwiches for a midday snack. His journey took one hour, and by the time he'd stopped to rest on the banks of the River Colne, his mental wellbeing had improved significantly. He spent the next thirty minutes idly watching passersby when suddenly his thoughts returned to the girl who'd occupied his mind the previous day.

Unable to explain why he seemed incapable of moving on, he remembered his father's advice before starting work. "Never be afraid to ask questions, Ben. It's a great way of learning, not an admission of ignorance. If you need help or guidance, ask someone older or wiser than you. Remember, many things can be taught in a classroom, but experience is not one of them. Naturally, you should only seek advice from people you respect, and even then, it's up to you whether to follow it. Ultimately, we're all responsible for our actions."

Though Ben had always respected his father, he realized that, in this instance, he'd not taken advantage of the guidance he'd been given. So, prior to arriving back home, he resolved to correct that at the earliest opportunity.

During his journey to work on Monday morning, Ben recounted the commitment he'd made the previous day, and in the process of doing so, he realized his supervisor was a man he held in high regard. *Would Bob Haskins*, he asked himself, *be someone who could give me advice regarding the girl who worked at the café?* Undoubtedly, he would be a perfect candidate to discuss work problems with, but matters of the heart, wasn't he too old to know about such things? At the same time, he'd heard from several co-workers that Bob Haskins was a happily married man, so despite his age, perhaps he knew something about relationships and romance after all. Figuring that he really had nothing to lose, Ben approached Mr. Haskins when the opportunity presented itself, which it did immediately after the lunch break that day. "Excuse me, sir," Ben said when they were out of earshot of the other workers. "What is it, Ben?"

"When it's convenient, I'd like to discuss a personal matter with you," Ben said sheepishly.

Bob Haskins frowned, "Very well, meet me in the rest area five minutes after the final whistle blows this afternoon."

"So, what is it you want to talk about?" Bob said when he arrived in the rest area.

Ben cleared his throat, "I'm hoping this doesn't sound trivial, as I don't want to waste your time."

"Let me be the judge of that. Now, kindly tell me what's on your mind, as I don't have all day." Bob responded firmly.

"Well, it's concerning a girl."

"Okay, I know relationships can be challenging. If you tell me more about what's going on, I'll try to help if I can," Bob said in a more conciliatory tone.

Ben gathered his thoughts, "I went to the station café to buy a sandwich last week. The girl who served me was," Ben stopped mid-sentence, trying hard to ensure the words forming in his mind were coherent.

"Carry on." Bob Hoskins said gently, attempting to encourage his young apprentice and put him at ease.

"Well, I was very attracted to her even though I'm unsure why. Because of that, I'd really like to make her acquaintance, but frankly, I do not know how best to do it."

"Did you talk with her at all?"

"Not really. I just gave her my order and paid the bill when she handed me the sandwich."

"Do you know her name or where she lives?"

"I'm afraid not. All I can tell you is that she has red curly hair, blue eyes, and freckles." Ben replied, realizing that his story was starting to sound pitiful.

Bob Haskins clasped his hands, "Well, Ben, let me give the matter some thought. I'll let you know if I come up with any ideas." He said as he set off for home.

For the first time since starting work, Ben stopped off at the Red Lion Inn for a pint on his way home. With a beer in hand, he mulled over his current situation, wondering if he'd marred his relationship with Bob Haskins in addition to his recent infatuation. Additionally, though he didn't think Bob was a gossip, it was now possible that his story of woe would be passed around to co-workers, and heaven knows what the repercussions of that might entail.

On his journey to work the following day, Ben made a decision. While his mood hadn't improved much, he believed his thinking was clearer. He would put the girl from the café out of his mind once and for all and never discuss her again with anyone, especially Bob Haskins. He didn't think the latter would be difficult, as he was certain his foreman had already dismissed his hair-brained story as part of the sometimes-illogical process of adolescence and would never give it another thought.

Ben kept a low profile for the rest of the work week, and by the time Friday rolled around, his frame of mind had improved to the point where he was looking forward to meeting up with friends on Saturday evening. On hearing the whistle blow to signal the end of the workday, he packed his tools and took them to the locker room when suddenly he felt a tap on his shoulder. "Let's meet at the pub in ten minutes. I have something to tell you," Bob Haskins said.

Ben was waiting nervously at a corner table when his foreman arrived carrying two pints of bitter ale. "I have some good news for you, young man." Bob said, "The manager at the station café is a neighbor of mine. I bumped into him on Wednesday evening at the Trades and Labor Club. I raised the subject of the young girl who works for him. Her name is Betty, and she lives in Old Hatfield, only a stone's throw from the café. She's been working there as a server since leaving school, and before that, she cleaned tables on Saturdays. My neighbor said that Betty is a sweet and intelligent young lady though sometimes a little shy. But let me get to the important bit. She remembers you coming into the café and is willing to meet you for a cup of tea at noon tomorrow."

It took Ben several seconds to digest the message, but when it sank in, he stood up and said gleefully, "Thank you, Mister Hoskins, thank you so much. I can't tell you how much I appreciate your help."

Ben barely slept a wink on Friday night though he was full of energy when his alarm clock started ringing. The previous evening, he'd set aside clean trousers and a fresh shirt to look respectable for his upcoming lunchtime meeting. Bob Haskins had told him that he'd be allowed to leave twenty minutes before the regular end of the workday, which would give him enough time to freshen up, change clothes, and cycle to the café in time for his noon rendezvous. "This,"

Bob said jokingly, "is part of the morale-boosting apprenticeship program."

Ben arrived at work early on Saturday, and to acknowledge his foreman's generosity, he worked through the morning tea break. Though not a word was spoken, Ben's gesture didn't go unnoticed, as at half past eleven, he felt a tap on his shoulder, "Time to get going, young man. It wouldn't be wise to show up late on a first date," Bob Haskins said through a wry smile.

Elizabeth (Betty) Williamson was born on October 19, 1920, in Hatfield, Hertfordshire, the second child of Charlie and Kathleen Williamson. Charlie worked as a firefighter while Kathleen was a full-time housewife and mother though she took a part-time cleaning job after her daughters started school. Betty and her elder sister, Dorothy (Dolly), were like minded, even though their personalities were quite different. Whereas Dolly was outgoing, Betty had a more reserved nature.

In 1932, Charlie Williamson was promoted to fire captain. While the country was still suffering from an economic depression, Charlie's increase in salary enabled him to provide his family with the bare essentials and the occasional little treat, unlike many less fortunate people. But alas, the fickle fingers of fate were looming. It began on a Thursday afternoon in early November when Charlie's station received a call alerting them to a fire at a local factory. On arrival at the scene, the security guard briefed Charlie on the status. The workers on the factory floor had already been evacuated, but the fire trapped several office personnel on the second floor because it engulfed the stairway. After quickly reviewing the layout of the building, Charlie determined that the best approach was for him and two of his crew to cut a hole in the roof, thereby providing an escape route for the people trapped in their offices. The crew was making good progress hacking their way through the structure when suddenly they heard a loud explosion, following which a large section of the roof collapsed, sending Charlie and his crew hurtling into the inferno below.

Charlie's unfortunate passing had a devastating blow on his wife, Kathleen, and while, for the sake of her daughters, she tried her best to hide her sorrow, she could never regain the zest for life that she'd previously enjoyed.

Shortly after commencing her final school year, Dolly decided that she wanted to become a nurse, and the following September, she enrolled as a resident student at a London hospital. At the same time, Betty secured a Saturday job at the local café, cleaning tables and washing dishes. Though this only produced a modest income, it helped her mother with the household expenses, as she struggled to maintain the family on a widow's pension.

With Dolly living away from home, Kathleen increasingly relied on Betty to help with chores, as in addition to her emotional decline, her situation was taking a toll on her physical wellbeing. Though Betty was more than willing to help her mother, it limited her time to devote to her school homework and largely prevented her from pursuing social activities.

In 1935, Betty left school, and given that she'd had minimal opportunity to search for employment, she gladly accepted the café managers' offer to expand her Saturday job into a full-time role.

Betty had been working at the café for a little over a year. During that time, she became increasingly frustrated by an absence of any social life and, specifically, interactions with boys her age—something that was increasingly on her mind. While most customers at the café were males, the majority were significantly older than Betty, and those of a similar age largely made inappropriate comments, normally with underlying sexual connotations.

Subsequently, Betty, though only sixteen years of age, began to wonder if she would end up living the life of a spinster. But the events that started one Friday lunchtime quickly turned her life in a new direction. Betty had been busy working at the counter, making sandwiches to order. She was in the process of serving a customer when she happened to glance at the next in line, only to find herself making eye contact with a young man who appeared to be entranced by her presence. And though the ensuing conversation simply entailed a request for a sandwich, there was something about the customer's shy and polite demeanor that she found attractive. Thinking, however, that the brief encounter was a one-off event because she'd never seen that customer before, she was excited when the manager told her later in the week that the same young man was interested in meeting with her.

After receiving permission to leave work early, Ben quickly washed his hands and face, changed into fresh clothes, and set off to the café, where he arrived a few minutes before his scheduled noon rendezvous. Having secured his bicycle on its stand, he took a quick peek through the café window, where he spotted Betty sitting at a table set with a white teapot and two mugs. Not wanting her to catch him spying, he promptly entered the front door and walked over to where she awaited him. "Hello, Betty," he said. "I'm Ben, and I'd like to thank you for allowing me to join you today."

Betty smiled sweetly, a gesture that had the same effect on Ben as it had when he last saw her. "It's my pleasure, Ben. Please take a seat and allow me to pour the tea," she said.

At first, the conversation was rather stilted, as the young couple only exchanged information on their respective workplaces and families. But in short order, the ice began to melt, and they soon moved on to more interesting subjects, which, in turn, were increasingly punctuated by outbursts of laughter. And there hadn't been a single break in the conversation until Betty happened to glance at the clock hanging on the café wall. "Goodness," she said out loud, "Look at the time. It's nearly two o'clock. I hate to bring our meeting to an end, Ben, but my mother will be waiting for me to take her on our weekly shopping trip, so I must run. But I really did enjoy meeting with you."

"Me, too," Ben said as he got up from his chair and escorted Betty to the front door. Not wanting to miss the opportunity, he said, "Betty, would you like to get together again?"

"Yes, I would like that very much," she said sincerely.

"What about tomorrow? Perhaps we could go for a walk." Ben said excitedly, hoping he wasn't being too pushy.

Betty stopped and turned to face Ben, "Okay, I'll meet you back on this very spot at two o'clock tomorrow afternoon," she said before giving him an unexpected peck on his cheek and then skipping glee-fully away, wearing a broad smile.

His Sunday date went even better than Ben could have imagined, and when he said goodbye at six o'clock that evening, he felt as though he'd known Betty forever. Their first date quickly led to the couple meeting two or three times each week, and in less than six months of courtship, they were joined at the hip. As a bonus, their relationship was met with the approval of their families and close friends, so it did not surprise anyone that on July 12, 1938, precisely one year after their first meeting, Ben proposed marriage—a request that Betty enthusiastically accepted.

On Saturday, October 15, 1938, Ben and Betty tied the knot at an afternoon ceremony held in St. Etheldreda's

Church, Old Hatfield, and this was followed by a reception at the Trades and Labor Club, a venue arranged by Bob Haskins and hosted by Betty's mother, who, along with her other daughter, Dorothy, provided the buffet-style catering. The fare consisted of egg sandwiches, corn beef with brown bread, fruit salad, and a homemade sponge wedding cake that had been iced and elaborately decorated with marzipan flowers by Bob Haskins' wife, Ada.

Additionally, Ben's parents provided white wine and orange juice for the traditional toast. Ben's closest friend, John, was the best man, and he gave a hilarious speech, part of which was making fun of both the groom and himself, primarily based on their childhood misadventures. Ben gave a touching response, thanking all for attending while paying particular thanks to his parents, grandparents, and Betty's mother. He ended on a lighter note, telling the tale of how forgetting to set his alarm clock one morning had led to him meeting Betty in the first place—a story that led to hearty laughter from all present. He also added a word of thanks to Bob Haskins for mentoring him at his workplace and arranging his first date with Betty.

At the conclusion of the reception, Ben and his new bride set off to enjoy the wedding present Ben's parents had given them, four nights at a bed-and-breakfast facility in the town of Rye.

Chapter Eight

Upon returning from an idyllic honeymoon, Ben Hollingsworth and his wife, Betty, moved into Betty's mother's home, where the spare bedroom had been temporarily converted into a bed-sit. They also registered with the local council, hoping to get their own home within a year or two.

Married life was instant bliss for the newlyweds, and much of their free time was spent discussing the future, with high priority given to starting a family. But the events unfolding in Europe caused them to delay their plans until the outlook became clearer. While they remained optimistic that Great Britain would ultimately be able to avoid a conflict with Adolf Hitler, their prayers were dashed on September 3, 1939, when the British Prime Minister, Neville Chamberlain, said in his radio address, "I have to tell you now that no such undertaking has been received and that subsequently, this country is at war with Germany."

Within days of hearing the Prime Minister's announcement, Ben was notified of the national conscription program, and the following February, he was instructed to report for basic training at the army base in the city of Aldershot. With Ben's absence, Betty began to experience bouts of anxiety, and this quickly developed into difficulties with her sleeping. Regrettably, matters only worsened when her sister, Dorothy, took a full-time job in London to further her nursing career. Thinking that her problems were likely a result of loneliness, Betty started a part-time evening job bartending at a local pub. At first, this seemed to help, but in reality, it was the beginning of another issue that gradually surfaced over the following months. Betty had never been one to drink alcohol; in fact, she could count the number of times she'd done so on one hand. But an offer from the pub manager to try a gin and tonic on the house one evening slowly turned into a regular event.

Despite the difficulties she was dealing with, Betty's mood improved each time Ben came home on leave. But her downs worsened when he returned to duty—as did her drinking habits.

In March 1942, Ben received notification of his imminent deployment to the Eighth Army, the military unit participating in the Western Desert Campaign. He used the rest of his leave to take Betty on a sentimental trip to Rye, where they'd honeymooned nearly four years earlier. Ben was encouraged by the improvement in his wife's positive attitude and her general enthusiasm, but within days of his departure, Betty's spirit slowly deteriorated again. While Betty's mother had helped her daughter through the daily challenges of wartime, they also caught up with her. One Tuesday, when Betty returned home from her job at the café, she found her mother lying unconscious on the kitchen floor. In a panic, Betty ran to the nearest telephone box to call 999.

Following two stressful hours in the hospital, during which Betty walked the circumference of the visitor's room more times than she could remember, a nurse arrived and led her to the consultation room. The doctor did his best to break the news as gently as possible, but when Betty discovered her mother was paralyzed on one side and had lost 70 percent of her eyesight, she broke down weeping.

On hearing the tragic news, Betty's older sister, Dorothy, took a week's leave to visit with her mother and help comfort her sister. Regrettably, her mother's outlook wasn't encouraging, and being in the medical profession herself, Dorothy knew there was no realistic possibility of her mother ever returning home. She tried her best to comfort Betty and would have stayed longer, but she was duty bound to return to her place of work, as casualties were arriving from the battlefields daily.

With long-distance encouragement from her sister, Betty tried hard to keep her spirits up, spurred on by wanting to do so for her and Ben's wellbeing. For several weeks, she found her mood improving a little, and though she was now consuming at least two alcoholic drinks each day, she felt certain that she could do without when the war was over, and things returned to normal.

In August of 1942, Betty was beginning to get excited at the prospect of her husband returning home, as she'd been told he'd get an extended leave following six months in action. Her excitement reached fever pitch when she saw the brown envelope marked "Official Government Document" that had just been slipped through her letterbox. Immediately, she grabbed it and tore it open, bursting with anticipation. But when she'd finished reading the opening paragraph, she slowly dropped to her knees, wishing she, along with her husband, was now dead.

Chapter Nine

Life without Ben seemed pointless to Betty, and before long, it was only the alcohol that kept her going. She visited her mother occasionally, but seeing her deteriorating condition made matters worse. The café manager where she worked was deeply sympathetic to her situation. Still, after enduring numerous instances of Betty failing to show up or arriving too hungover to function properly, he reluctantly let her go. And while she had just about fulfilled her evening duties as a barmaid, she was always inebriated by the time the final bell rang.

The arrival of 1943 brought about another step in Betty's decline when, reluctantly, the pub manager terminated her employment. Her termination resulted from a disastrous evening during which she'd spilled drinks on two customers, mistakenly poured gin instead of vodka, and, finally, dropped and smashed a bottle of ten-year-old scotch. Her dismissal brought about a new challenge for she now had less income and no longer had access to free drinks.

Trying to survive solely on a widow's pension was proving extremely difficult for Betty, and the little savings she'd had were disappearing rapidly. During an evening visit to a local pub, she shared her problems with a man named David, whose acquaintance she'd made when working at the café. "You know, Betty, I'd be happy to take you out for drinks whenever you'd like to." He said after listening to her predicament. "Thanks, David. That's very kind of you. But if I took up your offer, that would be rather selfish on my part, as there's no way I could ever reciprocate," Betty said.

"Don't worry about that," David said. "I make good money working as an electrician, and in any event, I'd enjoy your company."

Betty hesitated, for while she didn't want to take advantage of someone she barely knew, she didn't want to look a gift horse in the mouth. "How about a compromise," she eventually said. "Why don't you take me out this Friday evening, and after that, we'll just see how things go."

"You have a deal," David said excitedly. "Why don't I pick you up at six o'clock, and then I'll take you to a nice country pub?"

Betty was looking out the window of her front parlor when she spotted a black Ford Prefect pull up with David at the wheel. While she had little interest in a romantic involvement, as she believed her love for

Ben to be irreplaceable, she was looking forward to spending an evening at a pub and having a few drinks.

Their drive took approximately fifteen minutes, and as David had accurately described, the facility was in a beautiful, wooded area, and the interior décor had a charming Victorian theme. Furthermore, based on their reception, it was clear that David was a regular.

As the evening progressed, Betty slowly realized that she had little in common with David though he seemed nice enough. Notwithstanding the dullness of the conversation, she was still enjoying herself though this was largely an outcome of finishing up her third gin and tonic. "Ready for another one?" David asked as he swallowed the remaining drops of his brown ale. "Or perhaps you'd like to try something else."

"Any suggestions," Betty said.

"Well, I'm moving onto scotch if you want to join me."

"Sure, I'll give it a try," Betty said, in a frame of mind where more alcohol was the most important consideration, irrespective of its form. David ordered two doubles. When they were delivered, he distracted Betty momentarily, allowing him to pour some from his glass into Betty's without her noticing. He then proposed a toast and downed his drink in one gulp while encouraging Betty to do the same.

David's attention turned to gauging Betty's physical wellbeing as the conversation continued. While he wanted her to reach a point where she had lost all her inhibitions and powers of reasoning, he didn't want her to lose consciousness. His judgement told him that one more single scotch would likely do the trick.

Waking up with a hangover had long since been an experience Betty was familiar with. And Saturday morning was no exception. Betty lay with her eyes closed as her mind slowly engaged, praying that the throbbing in her head would soon subside. Her thoughts turned to the previous evening. She remembered drinking scotch though what took place after that was a complete blank. Gradually her headache eased, and she thought it best to get up and make tea, knowing this usually helped her recover. She was overcome with a strange feeling when she opened her eyes. Sitting up more quickly than usual, she was startled to find herself completely naked, and as her vision focused, she realized she was in unfamiliar surroundings.

"Oh, you've woken up at long last," David said as he came through the bedroom door, offering a glass of water.

"What am I doing here?" Betty shouted as her predicament began to register.

David placed his hands on his hips, tilted his head to one side, and said sarcastically, "Well, what do you think?"

Betty paused, struggling to arrange the words swirling around in her head. "I think you bloody well took advantage of me last evening. That's what I think," she said, mimicking David's tone.

"That's rich coming from you. But I must give you credit; you certainly know how to please a man!" David said through a thin smile.

Betty was dumbfounded. *Could I have possibly initiated sexual intercourse with someone I hardly knew?*

She asked herself. It didn't seem likely, but try as she might, she couldn't remember leaving the pub, let alone what had happened later at David's house. Suddenly, another thought flashed through her brain, which scared her profoundly. David correctly interpreted her facial expression. "What is it? What's bothering you?" He asked.

Betty struggled to answer, finally mumbling, "Did you—you know—cum in me?" She said as her face turned bright red.

Recognizing the reason for Betty's concern, David said, "No need to worry, love. I used a condom because I'm certain neither of us want you to get pregnant."

A look of relief spread across Betty's face, and despite the circumstances, she even managed a smile.

"Actually, I've got another one here," David said, picking up a plastic packet from the bedside table while removing his dressing gown.

Back in her home on Saturday afternoon, Betty promised herself she would never repeat the episode she'd gone through the previous evening. And as David had left her with four shillings for spending money, she could enjoy Saturday evening at the pub on her own. Sunday, however, came a day of reckoning because after counting the money she had left in her purse, she realized she had a choice to make. Given that she couldn't collect her widow's pension until Thursday morning, she could spend three nights drinking at the pub and not eat, or vice versa. After mulling over these options for over an hour, she finally decided to rescind the promise she'd made earlier. And at six o'clock, David escorted her to another evening at the pub.

While Betty had originally convinced herself that her time with David was nothing more than a one-off dalliance, the routine soon became a habit. And before long, this habit wasn't limited to only David. As word spread, Betty found herself with an increasing number of suiters willing to finance her cravings, knowing that she was prepared to pay them back in kind—an exchange that would have been unthinkable to her in times past.

One Friday evening, when Betty arrived at her local, she spotted four young men sitting at a table. One of them was a man named Brian, who she recognized from a date she'd had several weeks prior. When Brian saw Betty, he invited her to join his group, and following a kiss on the cheek, he introduced her to his companions, one of whom was his cousin, Ian. The conversation and the alcohol flowed freely, and Betty found herself feeling somewhat attracted to Ian in the process. It wasn't so much his looks. Though he had big brown eyes and a compelling smile, Betty sensed his vulnerability, a quality she inwardly related to. By the time Betty finished her fourth drink of the evening, two of Brian's friends had left, so she found herself talking almost entirely with Ian, as Brian had started a conversation with a man at the adjacent table. "Are you ready for a refill, Betty? It's my round," Ian asked.

"Yes, please," Betty replied with a smile.

Ian picked up the empties before standing up and heading off to the bar, which caused Betty to stare in disbelief momentarily. However, she thought she could regain her composure before the people around her took notice of her involuntary reaction. But that didn't apply to Brian, who picked up on it immediately, along with the probable cause. With his cousin out of earshot, he whispered, "Sorry, I didn't mention earlier that my cousin is a dwarf. He's rather sensitive about the subject, so I never talk about it in his company."

Betty was still recovering from the shock of talking with someone she'd assumed average height before witnessing him at four feet six inches tall. "Does he lead a normal life?" Betty asked, immediately regretting her poor choice of words.

"By and large, I'd say the answer is yes. Obviously, some things challenge him physically, but because of who and what he is, he's also had some interesting jobs. He had a couple of bit roles in the theater, and more recently, he worked as a circus clown. Though we best change the subject, Betty, as he's coming back with our drinks," Brian said, looking over his shoulder and spotting his cousin working his way through the crowd.

Saturday morning brought about what had now become a regular morning ritual for Betty. On regaining consciousness, which typically occurred between nine and ten o'clock, she would lie still with her head barely above the covers. This practice allowed her to reflect on the previous evening and let her hangover subside slightly. This morning, her mind wandered to events in the pub, specifically her reaction after discovering that Ian was a dwarf. *Why hadn't I noticed earlier?* she asked herself. She thought, probably because she only had a view of his head and shoulders, given that the pub tables were taller than average. But why didn't she notice that his arms were shorter than most? Maybe they were disguised by the jacket he was wearing.

The more she thought about Ian, the more her emotions swayed back and forth. There was a side of him she found warm and comfortable. But when she finally saw him standing up, with his stunted body and short, chubby legs, it made her feel uncomfortable. She asked herself, *Am I a bad and uncaring person for having such thoughts about someone who just happens to have physical differences from most people?* She didn't like the probable answer to her question, so she forced herself to think about other things.

In the act of doing so, she had a vague recollection of getting into bed with somebody the previous evening. *It must have been Brian*, she told herself, no longer surprised at behavior that would have brought her late mother to tears if she'd known what would become of her daughter. Thinking of Brian made Betty turn to look at the chair beside her bed, wondering if he'd left anything for her. She smiled when she saw a bottle of gin and two half-crown pieces together with a note. But her smile was quickly replaced with a grimace, followed by a bitter taste in her stomach when she picked up the note that read:

> *Thanks for a wonderful time, Betty.*
> *Love, Ian*

Coming to terms with the reality that she'd slept with Ian initially acted as a wake-up call for Betty. While she held no prejudice about him being a small person, having sex with him made her feel like she'd finally hit rock bottom. During the weeks following, she cut back on her drinking. However, given her circumstances, she eventually rationalized her consumption as justified and slowly reverted to past habits.

While the arrival of 1944 brought encouraging news for Great Britain and its allies in their war against Germany, Betty's depression and anxiety reached even greater depths. On one occasion, she seriously considered taking her life. But such thoughts were put to rest when, following a routine visit with her doctor, she discovered that by doing so, she would not only be killing herself but also another person—as she was pregnant!

On August 27, 1944, Betty gave birth to a four-pound baby boy named Roger. And given the circumstances of her pregnancy, she felt it disrespectful to pass on the family name of her late husband, so instead, she used her maiden name, Williamson.

During her pregnancy, Betty had attempted to contain her drinking, aware that by not doing so, she could adversely affect the wellbeing of her unborn baby. Shortly after Roger's birth, she slid back into her old habits. Like most mothers, Betty loved her child unconditionally, but given that she was frequently under the influence of alcohol, attention to her child's needs was often sorely lacking. At first, this only resulted in minor problems like forgetting feed times or not changing nappies, as her drinking caused her to sleep at random times during the day. But as Roger's mobility progressed, her increasingly frequent neglect resulted in more serious situations.

At age fourteen months, he fell off the sofa, resulting in significant bruising to his head and an ankle sprain, and shortly after his second birthday, a preventable accident nearly cost young Roger his life. It took place on October 9, 1946. Betty decided she and her young son would spend the day indoors during a particularly cold spell. Following Roger's mid-morning feed, she laid him on the sofa and covered him with a blanket to prepare for his midday nap. Then she put an extra shovel of coal on the fire and warmed herself up by consuming a large gin and tonic. As Roger lay sleeping beside her on the sofa, she had two more drinks before dozing off herself. Oblivious to the time that had passed, Betty was awoken by a piercing scream, only to find that her young son had walked across the room, tripped, and fallen headfirst into the fireplace, an event that could have been avoided if she'd remembered to replace the fire guard.

The trauma resulting from Roger's accident was extreme, and likely his death was only avoided by the excellent work of Doctor Cotter and his dedicated nursing team. Several surgeries, skin grafts, and intensive care allowed Roger to return home three months after his accident, but he'd carry the scars with him for the remainder of his life.

Roger's accident brought great pain and remorse to Betty, as she knew it was entirely her fault. While she badly wanted to make up for her negligence, she offered little or no resistance when her sister, Dorothy, strongly recommended that she and Roger move in with her.

Dorothy, known affectionately to her friends and relatives as Dolly, had completed her midwife duties in London, and after World War II, she returned to Hatfield. Consequently, while she couldn't watch out for Roger full-time, she could certainly support and encourage her sister and nephew.

Aunty Dolly, the name young Roger would eventually address her by, loved her nephew as if he were her own. She knew that the terrible scars covering seventy percent of his face would be a lifelong challenge for him but one that she remained optimistic he could overcome. Her hopes were dented, however, when it was discovered that he had yet another mountain to climb. During a routine hospital visit to check on his facial condition, the doctor advised that Roger had dwarfism and likely would only reach a height of around four feet six inches when fully grown.

News from Roger's hospital visit piled on the agony for his mother, and her drinking habits slowly took yet another turn for the worse. At the same time, it only increased Dolly's resolve. Besides caring for Roger's basic needs, she spent as much time as she could helping him develop his mental skills, knowing that achieving academic success would give him the best chance for a meaningful and hopefully successful future.

Dolly's dedication to Roger continued through his schooldays, and when he passed his eleven plus, the entry requirement to grammar school, her optimism for his future grew. Subsequently, thinking he would eventually study at a university, she was dumbfounded when one sunny day in June 1960, he told her that he'd left school to pursue a carpentry apprenticeship.

Chapter Ten

On Monday morning, Ricardo and Greta returned home from the shores of Lake Como, where they'd spent a weekend celebrating their first wedding anniversary while discussing their future.

It had been over two years since they escaped their awful existence in Sicily. Though they were anxiously awaiting the next stage of the arrangement with Mister Esposito, they were extremely grateful for the opportunity he'd given them.

While they'd known that they could never be completely immune from the mob's far-reaching tentacles for as long as they lived in Italy, Mister Esposito had taken steps to give them effective cover. These included arranging for Ricardo to have his shoulder-length black hair replaced with a crew cut and dyed brown and for Greta to have her wavy auburn hair straightened with blonde highlights added. Additionally, he'd provided them both with total wardrobe changes. Greta's outfits, previously consisting of flimsy and revealing dresses, were replaced by conservative outfits more typically worn by working-class women. In contrast, Ricardo's dark denim and leather outfits were substituted with casual linen suits in pastel colors. Mister Esposito had already christened Ricardo as Dickson at their first meeting, and following Greta's arrival, he'd renamed her Bianca as a tribute to her mother. "We've been so lucky to have met Mister Esposito," Greta said. "He could easily have taken advantage of our circumstances, but he never has. He's not a bully like the people who ruled our existence in Sicily. But at the same time, he's firm and direct, much like the women who ran the orphanage I was taken to. I respect those qualities, Ricardo, because I've found people who have them are nearly always straightforward and trustworthy. You said that Mister Esposito recently hinted at an opportunity for us to move outside of Italy when your work here is finished. Do you know where that might be or when such an event might occur?"

"As I've told you before, Greta, when Mister Esposito hired me, part of the deal I agreed to was carrying out a specific task. I don't have a set time for that, but the latest information he's given me suggests it will probably happen relatively soon. When I've completed that part of my agreement, I understand we will be offered an ongoing role in another location outside of Italy. Still, again, Mister Esposito hasn't yet been definitive in which country that might be."

"Ricardo, I know you've told me several times that you cannot disclose details of that part of your agreement, as you've given Mister Esposito your word that you would always keep it a secret. And, of course, I respect that. But I have a question. Might it involve doing something potentially dangerous to your physical wellbeing?"

Ricardo stopped to think for a moment. On the one hand, he would not breach the promise he'd made, but on the other hand, he didn't want to be untruthful to his wife if he could practically avoid doing so.

"I'm afraid I cannot answer that in good conscience. I just ask you to trust me. I can tell you, however, that there is a considerable upside to my carrying out his mission, assuming I complete it successfully. I'd prefer to wait for the right time to give you the details, and again, I must ask you to trust me on this one as well. Like you, I believe Mister Esposito is a man of his word, so I'm confident it will all work out for us in the long run."

"Ricardo, you know I trust you. I also respect that your word represents your honor. However, if carrying out Mister Esposito's mission could put your life in danger, given that you're now a married man, it's justifiable to refuse to do it. I realize that could put both of us in a very difficult position. But I'd rather we plan our escape, even if it means that we forfeit certain benefits and effectively start again from scratch because, my darling, I love you so much that I'd accept any lifestyle in preference to running the risk of losing you."

Ricardo took his wife into his arms and kissed her gently on the forehead, "My darling Greta, I know you are only looking out for my best interests, and I love you madly for that and so much more. But we both need to consider the bigger picture and the practicalities of our current situation. We both agree that Mister Esposito is a straightforward and honest man. However, I don't think he's a man who would take kindly to being double-crossed if you catch my drift."

"I'm not sure if I'm following you on this one," Greta said with a frown.

"In a nutshell, if Mister Esposito got wind that I was reneging on my word, it would be simple for him to severely punish both of us with just the stroke of a pen—so to speak."

"Now you've really lost me, Ricardo."

"Well, all he would need to do is tell the mafia who and where we are. And I'm certain that a man of his influence and contacts could do that with one quick phone call. And I'd never, ever do anything that would put you in that position," Ricardo said bluntly.

"My God, you're right! I didn't think the matter through. But I appreciate that you're looking ahead while always looking out for me, my darling." Greta said while embracing her beloved husband.

One Friday morning, a few weeks after celebrating his wedding anniversary at Lake Como, Ricardo Ferrante was dispatched to a wholesale distributor in Modena. For Ricardo, it was just a routine visit to a new customer who did not understand the basic rules of the game he'd decided to participate in.

"Where's Mister Martini?" Ricardo asked the young receptionist, who appeared to be preoccupied with filing her fingernails when he entered the front lobby of the distributors' offices.

"Do you have an appointment, sir?" the disinterested young lady eventually asked while turning her attention to renewing her lipstick.

"Last time I checked, this was a furniture distribution facility, not a beauty parlor. Now stop wasting my time and just tell me where Mister Martini is," Ricardo said bluntly.

Taken aback by her visitor's unexpected tone, the receptionist said nervously, "Well, his office is the second door on the right. But he's in a meeting now. If you give me your name, I'll try to find out when he's available."

Much to the receptionist's chagrin, Ricardo ignored her offer, and she watched in disbelief as her visitor strutted down the corridor and, without first knocking, flung open the door to Mister Martini's office before disappearing inside.

Mister Martini was dictating a letter to his secretary, an elderly gray-haired lady, when Ricardo curtly arrived. "Who the hell are you?" Mister Martini shouted upon seeing his uninvited guest. "You can't just barge in here. Now get out immediately, or I'll call security."

Ricardo stared at Mister Martini in silence for a few moments. "Call who you like," Ricardo eventually said, tossing a calling card onto Mister Martini's desk. "I'm here to remind you that you're two months behind on payments owed. We don't tolerate this kind of negligence, so I suggest you get the money transferred immediately. We wouldn't want something tragic to happen to your wife, Jovani, would we?"

Mister Martini's jaw dropped, and his face turned ashen, prompting Ricardo to add, "Nice to meet you, Mister Martini, and I trust there will be no need for me to visit you again."

Ricardo had just left his meeting with Mister Martini when his mobile phone rang. "Hello, Mister Dickson. I'm calling on behalf of Mister Esposito. He'd like you to join him for a noon lunch meeting today at Angelino's restaurant," Maria Bruno said.

Ricardo had long since learned that any directive from Antonio Esposito never contemplated rearrangement or impossibility. Based on that knowledge, he said, "I'm on my way," before jumping into his car and accelerating back onto the highway that led to Milan. During his journey, Ricardo speculated why his boss wanted to see him on such short notice. While he'd grown accustomed to receiving instructions at all times of the day and night, this last request sounded important, given that Mister Esposito knew his whereabouts, and he'd only ever been invited to Angelino's on one previous occasion.

Ricardo was relieved when he pulled up outside the restaurant with minutes to spare. Though unlike his only other visit years prior, the doorman greeted him warmly this time. "Good day, Mister Dickson. Mister Esposito is waiting for you at his usual table," he said, leading Ricardo across the dining room to the private booth where Antonio was sitting alone.

When the two men finished eating the lamb they'd ordered, washed down with a glass of Riesling, Antonio wiped his mouth with his napkin and placed his elbows on the table, "Dickson, I've invited you here today to update you on recent events. This morning, I completed the sale of my company. As you know, the key aspect of our agreement was for you to carry out a specific assignment of mine when the time was right. Well, that time is now. The details of what I need you to do and the corresponding travel arrangements are enclosed in this," Antonio said, handing Ricardo a sealed brown envelope.

"When you leave here, I want you to go to my home, collect my wife, and take her to the harbor in Genoa. I have some errands; I'll join her later this evening. First thing tomorrow morning, we'll board our yacht and head to South America. I expect it will take a few days to plan the mission I've asked you to undertake and likely several weeks to complete. When it's completed, contact me. You'll also find details of how to do that in the envelope. Then, assuming you still wish to move, I'll send my yacht to collect you and Greta to take you to your new home. And by the way," Antonia said, breaking into a rare smile, "There will be a check for $100,000 waiting for you when your work is finished."

Chapter Eleven

England

Weighing five pounds and six ounces, Samantha (Sam) Farmer was delivered by a local midwife at her parent's home in the outskirts of West London in 1932. Her father worked as a bricklayer, and her mother was a nurse.

Following Great Britain's declaration of war with Germany in 1939, Sam was evacuated to a village in Yorkshire. During this formative time, Sam met another evacuee, Sarah Gervais, who'd been transferred to the same neighborhood from her home in Kent. While the two girls had differing interests and backgrounds, they quickly became close friends and formed a special bond that would endure the test of time.

When Sam returned home at the end of 1945, she threw all her energy into schoolwork, as she'd already decided she wanted to become a teacher. Her academic accomplishments ran parallel to her unrelenting determination to reach her goal, so following graduation from the teachers' training college in South London, she secured a position at Trinity High School, where she would instruct English language and history.

Within weeks of taking up her job, Sam knew beyond doubt that she'd found the vocation she'd long since dreamt about, as her days were always pleasurable and fulfilling. Outside the classroom, Sam enjoyed an active social life, which included maintaining her friendship with Sarah, who, to Sam's surprise, had recently joined the police force. While Sam dated occasionally and certainly enjoyed the company of the opposite sex, she never built a relationship leading toward marriage.

As one of her admirers told her after they'd courted for several months, "Sam, you're a very attractive and lovely person. You have all the qualities of a woman I'd like to spend the rest of my life with. That being said, I think it's time for me to move on though I sincerely hope we can stay in touch and remain friends." To which a perplexed Sam replied, "I'm not sure if I'm following you, James. If you feel that way about me, why on earth do you want to end our relationship?"

"Because, my darling," James said, "For all intents and purposes, you're already married."

Sam hesitated momentarily, wondering if she'd missed the joke, as James often kidded around with her. Eventually, she said, "I'm a little confused. What makes you say that?"

James kissed Sam on the cheek while whispering in her ear, "It's because you're already married to Trinity High School."

At that moment, Sam had assumed James's statement to simply be a lame excuse to end the relationship, but as time passed, she realized that he had been correct in his assessment. Indeed, she was so devoted to her career and students that she would never have had enough time or energy to fit a husband, let alone offspring, into her busy life.

After eighteen years of outstanding service at Trinity High School, Sam was offered the girl's headmistress position.

Understandably, she was flattered because a promotion recognized her contributions to the school and offered a significant salary increase. But after due consideration, she reluctantly declined the offer, knowing that her heart lay in the satisfaction she derived from working each day with her beloved students.

Time passed quickly for Sam, and after completing thirty years of service, she knew the day she'd always been secretly dreading would arrive before too long. That day had the name *retirement* attached to it. And indeed, five years later, during a lunch break on a wet, cold day in March, the headmaster whispered in her ear, "Could you stop by my office at the end of your last lesson today, Sam? There's something we need to discuss." She was certain that her tenure with the school would end when the summer recess arrived.

"Take a seat, Sam," the headmaster said when she entered his study. "Sam, you've been with Trinity for thirty-five years now. During that time, you've served in a fashion that exemplifies all that is good about the teaching profession and much more, if I might say so."

Sam blushed and thanked the headmaster profusely. Though inwardly, she was hoping he'd get to the point before she burst into tears.

"There comes a time when all of us need to take the next step in our destiny," the headmaster continued, apparently oblivious that Sam's eyes were welling up. "As you know, we have two new staff members who joined us last year, and I believe they are ready to take a load off your shoulders."

The headmaster paused for a moment and smiled sweetly at the woman he'd grown to admire so much over the years. Sam took this opportunity to interject, sensing the headmaster was struggling to deliver his message. "Headmaster," Sam said, taking a deep breath, hoping it would prevent the moisture forming in her eyes from flowing down her cheeks. "I'm sure you are trying to let me down gently, but there's no reason to. I realized several years ago that I would have to reconcile myself to reaching this stage of my life, and now I just need to get on with it," Sam said, brushing away a tear with the sleeve of her blouse.

The headmaster's expression slowly turned from a smile to a look of mild confusion. "I'm sorry, Sam, but I think we might be talking at cross purposes. I was under the impression that when I offered you the girl's headmistress position, you turned it down because you always wanted to work closely with your students rather than be in an administrative role. Did I misunderstand?"

"No, you didn't," Sam responded, looking slightly perplexed.

"Perhaps I didn't explain myself fully. What I'm proposing is as follows. You continue in your current role until the summer break. Then, starting in September, I'd like you to undertake a mentorship role for our two new staff members until they feel comfortable. I'll leave it up to you to decide how long that will take though I'm assuming it won't be much beyond the Christmas break. This, of course, is just a precursor to what I have in mind for you in the longer term."

Sam sat up straight, waiting anxiously for what might come next.

"I know you've told me frequently that you try to keep in touch with past students and show an interest in their careers and family life. Well, I want this to become an area where Trinity breaks new ground. I want you to contact students who have graduated from Trinity and compile a scrapbook, so to speak, of their accomplishments. I'd also like you to provide an information center that would give past students a resource to get back in touch with old friends or classmates if they so wish and, perhaps, help them along with their careers.

"Finally, I'd like you to arrange periodic reunions by age. I suggest that these should be backdated as far as practical but, naturally, within the time frame of when you started at Trinity. This way, you'll likely have personal memories of the students involved. I should also mention that since you will not be teaching a curriculum, there is no effective retirement date. Consequently, you can work in this role for as long as you wish."

The headmaster paused, and a cheeky smile spread across his face. Having been born and raised in Glasgow, he occasionally adopted his native accent when he was in a lighthearted mood, "Just a wee guess, lassie, but I thought this arrangement might have some appeal?" Though a rhetorical question, it brought a wide smile to Sam's face.

What the headmaster had just outlined needed no further explanation, and in a rare moment of emotion overriding the normal thoughtful control of her words and actions, Sam jumped to her feet, threw her arms around the headmaster's shoulders, and kissed him zealously.

When September arrived, Sam went about her new role with the energy and enthusiasm a newly qualified teacher could only hope to emulate. To her delight, she could contact past students who still lived in the area, which, in turn, provided a resource to contact others. Sam's network slowly widened, as did its effectiveness, allowing her to act as either a coach or just as a friendly face for past students. By the end of the first year in her new role, Sam got the same level of satisfaction she'd gained from teaching class, something she'd previously believed impossible.

On returning for the new school year, Sam assembled a program that had been on her to-do list for some while—the arrangement of student reunions. She began with a twenty-five-year event, as she felt it might be too difficult to trace individuals from any further back. Consequently, this would entail contacting students from the upper sixth form of 1962 or those who'd left that class in either of the previous two years.

Fortunately, the school's archives had been well maintained, so establishing the names and addresses of students at the time of their leaving school was well documented. However, Sam quickly discovered that this information wasn't as helpful as she'd hoped because many parents of past students had moved without leaving forwarding addresses. But Sam was undaunted, in her usual manner, and by turning over every stone that could lead her to where she wanted to go, she eventually compiled contact possibilities for approximately sixty past students. This number was the trigger point for Sam, as she believed that if only fifty percent of those who had been located were to attend, it would still be a worthwhile event.

Over the ensuing days, Sam penned handwritten letters to every student on her list, inviting them to a class reunion scheduled to be held in the school gymnasium during the forthcoming summer recess. After mailing all the letters, Sam anxiously began checking her inbox the following week, keen to see what level of response she was getting.

It took nearly three weeks for Sam to receive the first reply, which, unfortunately, started with "I regret." But the following week, the first acceptance arrived, soon followed by several others. Each subsequent week brought encouraging news, that is, until she opened an envelope one Thursday morning. The note inside was from the mother of a class student from '62, an individual who'd already confirmed his attendance at the twenty-five-year reunion and a boy she remembered well. It read:

I regret to inform you that my beloved son was recently killed in a tragic work-related accident, so regrettably, he will not be attending your upcoming event.

Sam read the note repeatedly, praying that the words would magically change, but when reality finally hit home, her heart sank, leaving her feeling as if she'd lost a child of her own.

It took Sam several days to recover from the heartbreaking notification she'd received, during which she seriously considered cancelling the reunion event. But while she knew she would always carry a scar from the tragic news, she also believed it was her duty to the other students to keep moving forward.

Back at her desk, Sam threw herself into her work, focusing on building the former-student network and handling day-by-day matters concerning the first reunion. Keeping busy helped Sam's state of mind because while she knew the student tragedy was not of her making, she couldn't help feeling that she'd somehow created a not-meant-to-be moment.

With summer break approaching, Sam could celebrate confirmation from twenty-nine former students of their intention to attend the upcoming summer event, and there were still three weeks remaining to improve on that total.

When Sam was a young girl, her mother had often told her, "The sun always shines on the righteous," a phrase her mother truly believed applied to the daughter she adored. But despite the warm summer weather that Hatfield was enjoying, the sun chose not to shine on Sam at this particular time, for in the space of five short days, she received two more letters that left her completely disheartened and demoralized.

Feeling desperate to talk with someone with whom she could openly bare her soul, she contacted the person who she knew best fit that description.

"Hello, Sam, it's been a while. I hope you've been keeping well." Sarah Gervais called out to her longtime friend when she spotted her sitting in a corner booth of the wine bar.

"Lovely to see you as well, Sarah. It's been nearly seven months if my memory serves me correctly. I know we've both said this many times before, but we must try harder to meet up more often, as the days seem to pass quickly nowadays." Sam said, forcing a smile.

"You're right, of course. Both of us should try harder," Sarah said, leaning over the table to hug her friend. "I could tell from your phone call you had something on your mind that was upsetting you. Why don't I order us something to drink? Then you can tell me all about it."

"That sounds good," Sam said, prompting Sarah to summon the waitress and order two nine-ounce glasses of Cabernet.

The two women caught up on their general news while they waited for their order to arrive; after that, Sarah raised her glass in a toast. "I'm sure you have something important to tell me, but I'm in no hurry, so just take your time," Sarah said softly.

Sam appreciated her friend's ability to adapt to the moment, so she told Sarah every detail of the multiple tragedies that had occurred recently. She concluded by saying,

"Maybe I'm overthinking this, or I just haven't got my head on straight, but something about this whole picture doesn't sound or feel right, especially as the two boys were close friends. I know this might sound silly, but I can't help thinking that my arranging the twenty-five-year reunion somehow put a curse on the whole event, as nothing like this ever happened before I started this endeavor."

"First, Sam," Sarah said, adopting a slightly more formal tone, "Let me put you straight on one thing. The only reason your explanation may sound silly to you is because it is silly." Sarah paused, and her tone softened. "I can absolutely assure you that none of the tragedies have anything to do with you whatsoever. So, you must get that clear in your mind rather than drive yourself nuts by thinking that somehow you had a hand in any of it. I can also tell you, based on my thirty years of service in the police force, that coincidences occur from time to time; it's just a matter of the odds. That being said, it might help your frame of mind if we could satisfy ourselves that these were three separate incidents rather than there being a common thread, which is likely the reason you're blaming yourself."

Sam thought more clearly for the first time in weeks, which allowed her to relax a little. "Thank you, Sarah," Sam said softly, touching her friend lightly on the cheek. "Somehow, I knew you'd put this in perspective for me, and I'm very grateful. You said it would help if we could satisfy ourselves that these were three unrelated events, and I certainly agree. Do you have any ideas about how that could be accomplished?" Sam asked hopefully.

Sarah broke into a toothy smile that slowly spread from ear to ear. "Of course I do," she shouted aloud. "After all, I was a bleeding cop, you know!" she said, getting even louder and adopting an exaggerated cockney accent.

Sarah told Sam that though now retired, she continued to befriend several members of the force who were still active. Because of this, she was confident that she could dig up sufficient information to satisfy Sam that these were three separate and unrelated issues, and it was simply a coincidence that they all happened to members of the class of '62.

"It will probably take me a while to extract all the necessary information. But, by hook or by crook, I will get it," Sarah said, showing the steely determination that Sam had seen many times when the occasion warranted.

"I do not doubt that," Sam said, growing more confident that her dear friend would eventually put her mind at ease.

"One last thing," Sarah said.

"What's that?" Sam asked tentatively, as she'd learned over the years that when it came to her dear friend, one never knew what might come out of her mouth next.

"It's your bloody round!" Sarah shrieked, grabbing her empty glass and holding it up in the air for all around her to see.

Chapter Twelve

Four weeks had passed since Ricardo set off on Mister Esposito's special assignment. During this time, Greta tried her best to remain patient, knowing their future depended on her husband's success. Given the amount of free time available during his absence, she'd taken the opportunity to catch up on her reading and reflect on her hopes and wishes for the future.

Greta knew beyond doubt that she'd been extremely lucky to meet Ricardo, especially as it was a million-to-one shot any pimp would marry one of the prostitutes working under his charge and give her the freedom she'd largely given up hope of ever achieving.

In truth, when he first asked her to accompany him on his escape from Sicily, she had been more than a little skeptical about his true intentions. But at the time, joining him still seemed a favorable option than continuing with her dreadful existence in Messina. However, events had turned out far better than she could have imagined, as Ricardo had proven to be a loving, caring, and thoughtful individual.

The icing on the cake was when he proposed marriage one year after they arrived in Milan. The subsequent wedding was a private affair but an event that Greta found to be beautiful and romantic in its simplicity. Her only regret was that she could not share the occasion with her mother.

Ricardo had informed Greta that it was impractical to accurately predict a date for his return. Furthermore, it was unadvisable for him to contact her during his absence. But despite knowing this, Greta couldn't help but get a little anxious when six weeks of silence had passed. Additionally, though she clearly understood that Ricardo had sworn to keep the details of his mission a secret, her instincts told her it almost certainly involved a degree of danger. Consequently, she was greatly relieved when she answered an incoming phone call early one morning to find Ricardo on the line.

"I can't talk for long, my darling, as I still have some business to take care of. I'm currently in France, but if all goes well, I'll be with you in three or four days from now," he said.

"It's wonderful to hear from you, Ricardo," Greta said, letting out an involuntary sigh of relief. "I've missed you terribly. I know you must be very busy, and I don't want to hold you up. All I need to know is that you're safe and you'll be home soon."

"Everything's fine. Likewise, I miss you and can't wait to hold you in my arms again. I'll be there soon; I promise. But now I must be on my way."

The brief call was all Greta needed to raise her spirits and reinvigorate her, so she devoted all her energy to preparing a special welcome for Ricardo's return. Thinking of the things her husband would likely have missed the most during his absence, she ran to the store and purchased the ingredients for his favorite meal. Next, she stopped at the florist, where she bought displays of assorted flowers and a bunch of red roses. Finally, she visited a woman's clothing and fabrics store, where she acquired new lingerie and a set of sky-blue silk sheets.

Two days after her shopping expedition, Greta was taking a midday siesta when she was suddenly awoken by a noise from the hallway. At first, she was fearful, thinking that a burglar was entering her home. But when she peeked nervously around the bedroom door, she was elated to see Ricardo standing there. Though she hadn't planned for it to happen this way, she quickly realized that the see-through night dress she was wearing was having the effect on Ricardo that she hoped it would. In a heartbeat, she was wrapped in his arms, and moments later, the two of them were entwined between the new sky-blue silk sheets that adorned their bed.

Following an afternoon of passionate lovemaking, Greta washed and dressed before setting off to the kitchen to prepare dinner, allowing her husband ample time to take a leisurely shower and unpack his case before joining her. When Ricardo eventually arrived in the dining room, he was greeted with a glass of Chardonnay while seated at a table elaborately decorated with an assortment of flowers. Following a return trip to the kitchen, Greta reappeared carrying a dish of seafood risotto, which she set in the middle of the table.

"Salud," Ricardo said with a smile, touching Greta's glass with his.

"Likewise, my darling, and bon appetite," Greta responded, leaning across the table to kiss her husband after placing a large spoonful of risotto on his plate.

"Can you tell me a little about your trip? And what happens next?" She said after she'd swallowed her first forkful.

Ricardo hesitated, trying hard to find the correct words, "I suppose, most of all, I'm just thankful it's all over. It's not something that I would care to be involved with again, though. Fortunately, there's no reason to think I ever would be."

Greta felt certain that her husband had been through an unpleasant and probably painful experience. Furthermore, as he'd given his word to Mister Esposito that he'd always keep the details a secret, she would not press the subject any further. She also knew he'd sacrificed for their mutual benefit and was extremely grateful.

Recognizing that it would be a good time to change subjects, Greta said, "I would like to hear more about our future. Is now a good time to discuss it?"

"Yes, of course. I'm keen to give you an update. I spoke with Mister Esposito by phone last evening. Guess what? He's already arranged for us to move away and start a new life in South America. And to make things comfortable for us, we can travel there on his yacht. It's scheduled to arrive in Genoa in approximately three weeks. Mister Esposito is also arranging for our belongings to be packed and transported to the harbor. So, at long last, I will have ongoing employment, and we can start a life without looking over our shoulders because we'll finally be well outside the reach of any possible mafia influence."

Ricardo was tempted to tell Greta about the reward he would receive, as he'd never mentioned the subject before. But on second thought, he decided it would be better to wait until both the money was in his hands and the occasion was right.

Chapter Thirteen

At eight o'clock on a warm Wednesday morning, Greta and Ricardo finished loading their personal effects into the van they'd rented the previous day. All that was left for them to do was lock up the house and deliver the key to the property manager. Then they'd be ready for the two-hour drive to Genoa, where Mister Esposito's yacht was waiting to take them on their journey to freedom.

Shortly before noon, Ricardo pulled up at the harbor entrance gate, where he came face to face with a security guard. The individual was a tall, heavy-set man wearing a dark green uniform and sporting a thick mustache. "What's your business here?" he asked bluntly.

"We're guests of Mister Esposito," Ricardo replied a response that brought forth an immediate change in attitude.

"Drive down to the end of this road and turn left where you see the sign marked 'Docks.' Then proceed to pier number seven, where you'll find someone waiting for you," he politely said while raising the barrier preventing Ricardo's progress.

Following the guards' directions, Ricardo soon caught sight of a glorious white yacht with the words *Forget Me Not* emblazoned on its hull in bright-blue letters. When Ricardo pulled up next to the yacht's gangway, he was approached by a man wearing a white suit, black shoes, and a peaked cap decorated with braided yellow satin cord and embossed with shiny gold-colored rivets.

"You must be Mister Ferrante. And I'm guessing the beautiful lady sitting next to you is your wife. Allow me to introduce myself; I'm the ship's captain, Mario Enzo, and I'll be responsible for getting both of you safely to your destination. If you follow me, I'll show you to your quarters. You do not need to bring your luggage; I'll have my staff take care of that and the van." He said as he led Ricardo and Greta to a suite on the upper deck, offering a magnificent view of the Mediterranean Sea.

On arrival at the quarters that would serve as their home until they reached their destination, the captain gave Ricardo and Greta a brief overview of the journey ahead. It would be carried out in three stages: the first leg would take them to Freetown in Sierra Leone, the second leg to Jamaica, and the third and final leg to their ultimate destination, Rio de Janeiro—a revelation that thrilled both Ricardo and Greta, as Mister Esposito had only told them they would go to South America.

The captain further explained that the overall journey was expected to take twenty-five days, though there could be some minor variance due to weather or unforeseen delays in docking and re-launching. "I expect you'll want to get settled before finding out more about your temporary home. I'll send my second in command to visit you in one hour. He can answer any questions regarding your accommodations and then give you a tour of the ship's facilities. We'll be raising anchor and heading out at four o'clock this afternoon. Dinner will be served in the banquet room at half past seven. That will allow you to meet the other guests if you so wish. Alternatively, we can serve dinner in your suite. In the meantime, if you're hungry, you'll find your refrigerator stocked with various snacks. Please ask my deputy or me if you have questions during our journey." At this point, Captain Enzo saluted and took off to the wheelhouse.

Following a tour of the yacht, Ricardo and Greta spent a relaxing afternoon in their suite before changing into formal attire more suitable for dinner. Upon arriving at the banquet room, they were greeted by the captain and the chef, who introduced them to some other guests. When the meal was over, Ricardo and Greta briefly socialized with several other couples, finally retiring to their suite shortly after ten o'clock, exhausted but exhilarated from all that had transpired in the last twenty-four hours.

Ricardo and Greta spent most of the journey relaxing in their suite or sunbathing on the foredeck when the weather was warm. For meals, they ate snacks in their suite during the day but most nights took dinner in the banquet room. Though the Ferrante's enjoyed relaxing during the 7,000-mile trip, they were thrilled and relieved when early one Sunday morning, they spotted Mount Corcovado in the distance, with Christ the Redeemer resting majestically on its peak.

Shortly before noon on a sunny Tuesday morning, the *Forget Me Not* anchored at Pier Maua, a beautiful location that offered dramatic views of Copacabana Beach. Having thanked the captain and his crew for all their help, Ricardo and Greta disembarked to find a man wearing a blue tee shirt and green shorts holding up a signboard bearing their names.

"Good day to you both. Welcome to Brazil. My name is Duarte, and I'll take you to your new home. The crew will bring your luggage shortly, and when they've finished loading it," Duarte said, pointing at a white van parked on the opposite side of the road, "We'll be on our way. It should only take seventy-five minutes to reach our destination though, of course, it depends on traffic."

The Ferrante's journey took them through vast open fields punctuated by forested mountains until they eventually arrived at Paracambi. When the van came to a halt on the driveway of a cottage built out of clay, lime, and timber, Duarte disembarked to help Ricardo unload the luggage.

"Welcome to your new home. I hope you'll both be very happy living here. Mr. Esposito asked me to tell you that there's a note on the dining room table detailing all the information you need. He also said he'd be contacting you shortly. So, unless you have any questions, I'll be on my way." Duarte said.

"I'm sure Mr. Esposito's note will suffice," Ricardo responded. "Greta and I wanted to thank you for meeting us and bringing us here."

"You're very welcome," Duarte said, jumping back into the van and speeding off toward Rio.

After unlocking the front door to the cottage, Ricardo picked up his wife and carried her across the threshold. Traditionally a custom for newlyweds, Ricardo thought it appropriate for the current occasion, as they were effectively starting a new life together. Following a hot-blooded kiss, Greta said, "I can hardly believe we're here, Ricardo. We've come a long way since leaving Sicily, and I'm not only referring to the miles we've travelled. It's indeed taken three long years, but I already know it's all been worthwhile. Finally, we can settle down, and perhaps we can start planning the family we've discussed?"

"First of all, let's explore our new home and read the message from Mister Esposito. Then perhaps we can focus on our thoughts for the future," Ricardo replied, slowly running his hands up Greta's back and kissing her again.

The couple began their tour of the house, which, judging by the smell of fresh paint, had been recently decorated. When they finished surveying the ground floor, Greta jumped onto Ricardo's back with her arms locked around his neck while they slowly navigated the stairs. On reaching the top landing, Greta took Ricardo's hand, and they explored the remainder of their new home together. On re-entering the dining room, Ricardo picked up the envelope Mister Esposito had left for them, ripped it open, and read aloud:

Dickson,

I was pleased to receive your phone call several weeks ago, during which you confirmed that the mission I'd given you had been successfully completed. I trust that you and your wife had a pleasant journey and that you like your new home.

I've been satisfied with your work over the years, so I'm offering you continuing employment on the same terms as those we had in Milan. As for Greta, I'd like to continue having her plan and cook meals when I'm entertaining, but I also have other activities that may suit her talents. We can discuss this in more detail at the appropriate time.

You can live in the cottage, rent-free, as long as you continue in my employ. If you haven't inspected the garage, you'll find a truck for your business and personal use.

Finally, I'd like to invite both of you to join my wife and me for dinner at 6:00 p.m. this coming Saturday. The address and directions are on the enclosed card.

Welcome to Brazil,
Antonio Esposito

Following four exciting days of unpacking their belongings and getting familiar with the neighborhood at three o'clock on Saturday, Ricardo and Greta began preparing for the evening ahead. Given the warm weather, Ricardo wore a light-blue denim suit with a white open-neck shirt, while Greta sported a red linen dress that highlighted the pearl necklace Ricardo had given her as an engagement present. They'd been told the drive to Antonio's home would take approximately thirty-five minutes, but not wanting to be late for their six o'clock dinner, they gave themselves plenty of time.

Antonio's new home was on five acres of partially wooded land in a sparsely developed area. The entrance gate opened immediately upon Ricardo announcing his name at the intercom. By the time they'd driven down the long gravel road that led to the front door of the stucco-clad mansion, Antonia was already standing outside to greet them.

"Welcome to my home," Antonio said warmly, kissing Greta's hand before shaking Ricardo's. "Follow me," he said, leading them through the reception area and along a hallway to the dining room, where he introduced his wife. When the two couples had taken their seats, Antonio called for the waiter he'd hired for the evening, who handed out the menu that offered several options.

At Mister Esposito's recommendation, they all chose bobo de camarao as an appetizer, feijoada for mains, and tapioca crepes for dessert, and each course was paired with a suitable wine.

Before their arrival, Greta had been concerned that the formality of the evening might make it difficult for her to participate, and the fact that she'd never met Antonio's wife might enlarge that challenge. But her concern was soon put to rest, as both hosts went out of their way to include her in the conversation, irrespective of the discussed topic.

When the foursome had all finished dessert, Antonia changed the tone of the conversation. For the first time in the company of either Ricardo or Greta, he talked about his early life and how he started his business. He'd grown up in a working-class family, and upon leaving school, he used some of his spare time to repair or rebuild various household items that had been broken or damaged. This led him to take an interest in designing and making new furniture, which inspired him to enroll in evening classes at a technical school to learn more about the skills required.

During two years of part-time tuition, he designed and constructed several pieces of furniture and was subsequently given the opportunity to display them at an annual event the school arranged for public viewing. Traditionally, this exhibition was only attended by friends or relatives of the students. But on this occasion, a recently qualified interior architect was also present. He was sufficiently impressed with Antonio's handiwork, so he suggested Antonio pursue it as a business. He said that Milan would be a good choice to locate for such an endeavor, as designer furniture was very much in vogue there. While intrigued by the concept, Antonio initially thought it was out of his league. But the following year, he decided it was worth giving it a shot, and to his surprise and subsequent delight, the business took off.

When Antonio finished telling his story, he rose from his chair, an act that Ricardo and Greta assumed to be a signal the evening was concluding. But Antonio said, "Ricardo, there are some matters I'd like to discuss with you in private. So, I suggest we retire to my study. I'm sure the ladies will find plenty to talk about, which will probably include some subjects they'd prefer us not to hear," a statement that brought an immediate response from his wife. "That's very insightful of you, my dear," she said, glancing at Greta while chuckling aloud.

Having directed the hired waiting staff to bring Montecristo cigars and Remy Martin Louis XIII to his study, Antonia led Ricardo out from the dining room, along the passageway and into another room that had a mahogany desk at one end and a seating area at the other.

When both men had lit their cigars and tasted the cognac, Antonio sat back in his chair, looking thoughtful. "Dickson, there are a few things that I wanted to tell you, and I thought it best done in private. You've known me for three years, but in many ways, you don't really know me at all," he said, which caused Ricardo to sit up in his chair.

"I'm not going into specifics, but I wanted to express my general feelings about you."

Ricardo felt his back stiffen in anticipation.

"I've had an unusual life, and through it, I've learned to be suspicious of most people I meet. In fact, I've only ever known four people who I completely trust." Antonio paused and took another draw on his cigar. After exhaling, he continued, "And you, Dickson, are one of those four."

Antonio remained silent for several moments, leaving Ricardo unsure whether he was expected to respond.

"That quality means an awful lot to me. But I'm not going to say any more on the subject other than to tell you that if there is ever anything you need from me, don't hesitate to ask."

Antonio took another draw on his cigar. "There's something else I want to tell you about the mission you carried out for me. What I tell you should never be repeated for obvious reasons that don't need explaining. I have a certain characteristic that's hard to explain or perhaps even understand. Frankly, I'm not sure if I understand it myself—but in a nutshell, if someone crosses or embarrasses me, I find it impossible to ever forget about the matter or forgive the person involved."

After his statement, Antonio rose from his chair and pulled an envelope from his jacket pocket.

"One last thing," he said, "Inside this envelope is a check for $100,000 US dollars, the amount I promised to pay you when your mission was completed."

Having expressed their gratitude for a pleasant evening, Ricardo and Greta climbed into their truck and took off on the journey home. Greta waved through the rear window until they'd exited the driveway, at which point she immediately turned to Ricardo. "Okay, what did you make of the evening? And more importantly, why did Mister Esposito want to talk alone with you in his study?" She asked anxiously.

"I'm still trying to process some of this evening's conversations and events," Ricardo said. "Mister Esposito is a very unusual man. Like you, I believe him to be a good person and trustworthy, but he has some quirks. Also, one aspect of the evening struck me as bizarre beyond explanation. So, I suggest you allow me to think things through for a while; perhaps we can discuss this evening in the comfort of our home."

While Greta was dying to hear the details, she knew her husband liked carefully analyzing a situation before voicing an opinion. "Okay," she said reluctantly. "But will you please try to get me home as quickly as possible, or I might just blow a fuse!"

When Ricardo brought the truck to a halt outside their new home, Greta jumped out and ran straight to the bathroom. Given the hour of the day, she decided it would be more agreeable to talk in the comfort of their bed, so she quickly removed her makeup and changed into night attire before running into the bedroom, where Ricardo was already under the sheets awaiting her arrival.

Chapter Fourteen

"Come on then! Spill your guts, and don't sugar-coat anything, especially the bit you referred to as weird," Greta said, snuggling up close to her husband.

Ricardo scratched his head, "Well, actually, the really weird bit happened when we first arrived."

Greta's eyes opened wide, "Sorry, I don't know what you mean by that?" she said with a look of bemusement.

"Just meeting his wife was the weirdest bit."

"I didn't notice anything weird about his wife. I thought she was very nice!"

"I didn't say his wife was weird; I said meeting her was."

"You're not making any sense, Ricardo. How much cognac did you drink in Mister Esposito's study?"

"It's not the alcohol; I can assure you. It's just that the woman we met tonight wasn't the same woman I drove to Genoa a couple of months ago."

Greta gasped. "Are you sure?" she asked as her mind ran over explanations. "Maybe she's dyed her hair? Or perhaps she's had a facelift? Sometimes, people can look very different if you've only met them once," Greta continued.

"That may well be. But in this instance, I'm certain that the woman who introduced herself as Mister Esposito's wife when I drove her to Genoa was several inches taller than the woman we met this evening. Furthermore, she had a very voluptuous figure, whereas the woman we met tonight was slim. So, unless tonight's wife has had her legs shortened and shed fifty pounds in a matter of weeks, then yes, I'm sure it's not the same woman!" Ricardo said with purpose.

"No need to be sarcastic, dear. I was only exploring possibilities," Greta responded, chiding her husband.

"Sorry, I didn't mean to be rude. But my point is that I just can't make any sense of what possibly could have happened."

Greta felt the conversation was getting slightly out of hand, so she changed gears. "Let's talk about something else. What did Mister Esposito have to say when the two of you went to his study?"

Ricardo's facial expression quickly changed from a look of anguish to a warm smile. "He told me how much he appreciated our relationship. I'm having difficulty explaining myself because I sincerely believe Mister Esposito is a well-meaning and trustworthy man. But at the same time, there's something about him, or perhaps his past, that I can only describe as strange, or maybe eccentric would be a more appropriate term."

"I'm not sure I'm following you," Greta said with a frown.

"That's probably because I'm not really following myself. And I'm still struggling to find the words that match my feelings. I suppose what I'm trying to convey is that while I believe Mister Esposito to be a good person, he's someone I don't really understand and certainly a man I wouldn't want to get on the wrong side of. Does that make sense?"

"Sort of, I suppose. But there's no reason to think we'll ever get on his wrong side, right?" Greta asked though it was an abstract question that she wasn't expecting Ricardo to answer.

Ricardo thought it was time to change the subject, "So, I've told you my thoughts about the evening; what about yours?"

"Well, Mister Esposito and his wife were kind and charming. They certainly made me feel at home. What I found to be of particular interest was when Mister Esposito talked about his past and how he started his business. That's something I've never heard him do before. I also appreciated his wife's modesty and her sense of humor. And one thing struck me about her. Mister Esposito must be very talented to have built such a successful business. While his wealth might be an attraction to a certain materialistic type of woman, I'm sure his wife doesn't fit into that category. It's obvious that she's very bright, and I suspect she's been successful because of her efforts. She's also a very attractive woman.

"Consequently, I think it speaks volumes to see that she clearly is very much in love with Mister Esposito because of who he is rather than how much money he has. Frankly, I hope my words do not condemn females, but I don't think many women of her caliber would fall for someone at tops four-feet-seven-inches tall and has terrible scarring over much of his face!"

While agreeing with Greta's observations, Ricardo wanted to move on to the matter that he'd been dying to tell Greta for the last few hours. "By the way, darling, Mister Antonio gave us a welcoming present. It's sitting in the drawer of our bedside table. Would you like to see it?" Ricardo asked.

"Can't you just tell me what it is," Greta said, as she was feeling sleepy.

"It's a check for $100,000. So, while it may not be enough for us to retire on, it certainly gets us off to a darn good start," Ricardo said.

When Greta digested her husband's words, she let out a shriek of delight. "How on earth did I manage to find such a clever husband? Not only that, but I couldn't possibly think of a better note on which to finish our day," she said, tears of joy filling her eyes.

"That's funny because I could," Ricardo replied, as he began nibbling on Greta's ear lobe and running one hand up the inside of her thigh.

Epilogue

When Sarah Gervais returned home from the lunch meeting with her lifelong friend, she planned the investigatory work necessary to provide answers that hopefully put Sam's mind at ease.

Utilizing the determination and people skills that had enabled her to enjoy a successful career in the police force, she methodically met with past contacts and others familiar with the circumstances until she'd assembled a clear picture of the tragic outcomes for three students from the class of '62.

Margaret Carpenter left Trinity High after her fifth year, having received notice of failing to pass any of the O level exams she sat for. She secured her first job as a sales assistant in the high-end department store's women's clothing section, largely because of flirting with the store manager. Making the most of her looks and shapely figure, she could subsequently persuade the manager to give her another opportunity to become one of the young women who modelled the store's latest fashions on Saturday mornings. On such occasions, Margaret would try to wear the most revealing new outfits available, which eventually caught the eye of a modelling agency's representative.

Less than four years after leaving school, posters of Margaret wearing skimpy bikinis and provocative underwear hung on the walls of many of London's swinging-60s hotspots, making her a local celebrity.

With her upgraded status, Margaret quickly attracted several suitors, adding to her ever-growing ego. But she felt she'd hit the jackpot when the lead singer of a talented up-and-coming rock group named Mick invited her out on a date.

A weekend in Paris with Mick attracted paparazzi members, rapidly moving Margaret's social standing onto another level. But while Margaret had fallen head over heels in love, the feelings were not reciprocated, as Mick viewed her as just one of the many attractive women he could party with whenever he chose. And his idea of partying followed the mantra of the day for most popular rock singers: sex, drugs, rock 'n' roll.

While Margaret eventually picked up on Mick's indiscretions, she ignored them, hoping it was just a phase that would soon pass. But when Mick's behavior showed no sign of changing, instead of moving on, she naively decided that joining in with his habits would bring them closer together. Consequently, she participated in the drunken orgies that were a regular part of Mick's life. However, Margaret didn't foresee the trap that she was falling into, as in short order, she also became addicted to alcohol and cocaine. Unable to continue with her regular job, Margaret increasingly relied on financial support from Mick. She also moved into his apartment, believing they would marry one day. She became even more convinced this would be the outcome of discovering she was pregnant, something she proudly announced to Mick when he returned home from a two-week tour of Liverpool's nightclubs.

One week later, however, her world fell apart when, after waking up late on a Sunday morning with her usual hangover, she found a note on her bedside table that read:

Mags,

It was good while it lasted, but everything must end; I'm afraid. The boys and I have just signed a deal with an American promoter. By the time you read this note, we'll likely be up in the air on our way to Los Angeles.

Hope all works out for you.
Mick

P.S. And don't think I fell for any of your bullshit about it being my kid. I've heard that crap a thousand times before. By the way, rent on the flat is due next Wednesday if you want to continue staying there.

From that moment on, Margaret's existence rapidly spiraled even further downhill. Her parents were unsympathetic, believing she had made her bed and now must lie on it. And in short order, the savings she'd previously accumulated disappeared, along with most of the people she'd assumed to be her friends.

As increasing desperation crept into her life, heightened by the expense of purchasing the drugs and alcohol she now craved, Margaret sought the assistance of nightclub managers that had kissed up to her during her heyday. At first, this avenue provided a little relief, but when Margaret no longer had anything to offer, she was unceremoniously shown the door.

Fortunately, having a young child enabled Margaret to qualify for a small council flat in the town where she'd grown up, and when young Mick started school, she secured a part-time job as a shop assistant. Though she eventually managed to wean herself off the drugs, she never had the same success with alcohol. Consequently, her financial situation remained precarious until she accidentally discovered a recipe that helped to support her drinking habits. Margaret's neighbor was agreeable to looking out for young Mick on Friday and Saturday evenings. This allowed Margaret to visit her local pub, where she discovered there were male candidates who'd pick up her bill if she spent twenty minutes with them in the back seat of their car after closing time.

Young Mick had undistinguished academic success but became a very competent swimmer. As a result, after completing his fourth form school year, he secured a job as both an instructor and lifeguard though the opportunity required that he move to the south coast.

Living alone took a further toll on Margaret, whose existence became increasingly solitary, as most evenings, her only company was contained in a bottle. And by the time her forty-first birthday came around, Margaret was at her wit's end; that is, until one day, from out of the blue, she received an unexpected and unlikely expenses paid invitation to visit with someone from her distant past. Thinking this could be a turning point in her life, the following week, she boarded a

British Airways flight to Rome, advising her neighbor that she planned to return home in a few weeks.

While her neighbor knew Margaret's return date was flexible, she got concerned when six weeks passed, and Margaret had neither returned nor sent word of her whereabouts. Consequently, the following week, she reported the matter to the police though their subsequent investigation failed to produce any tangible results. Accordingly, Margaret remained on the official missing persons list until the following year—when her body was found washed up on a beach near Genoa. Following due process, the coroner's office ruled it as death by misadventure.

Bob Lane completed his fifth year at Trinity High after obtaining passing grades in five O-level subjects, including mathematics and English language. This qualified him to study at the Hertfordshire College of Building, where, two years later, he obtained a national diploma in construction management.

After completing his college work, Bob pursued a career with a large construction company, and upon receiving his first promotion, he married Jean, a girl he'd been courting for two years.

The Lanes had three children, and Jean was a stay-at-home mum while Bob focused on his career. Shortly after celebrating his fortieth birthday, Bob was promoted and assigned to manage the construction of a new twenty-story office building. The project was on schedule, and the concrete structure had risen to the twelfth floor.

Late one Thursday afternoon, Bob answered a knock on his office door to find two men dressed in business suits standing there. One of the men introduced himself as a senior design engineer from the company, supplying and installing the elevators. "I apologize for calling on you without prior notice, but please allow me to explain. This is Mister Bruno," he said, gesturing towards his companion. "Mister Bruno is the general manager of our Italian subsidiary, and he's been visiting with us to see how we operate here in London. We spent our day touring around the general locale, and suddenly, I remembered that we'd be starting work on your project shortly.

"Consequently, I thought we'd stop by on the off chance we may get to look around the site. Again, I apologize for not giving you advance notice, and knowing that it's getting late in the day, I fully understand if that's not possible."

Bob had long since learned that good relationships with suppliers and subcontractors were always beneficial, and in any event, leaving for home a few minutes later than normal was of little consequence, as it would give time for the commute traffic to ease. "My pleasure," Bob said, stopping by the adjacent office to brief his assistant before leading his guests to the passenger hoist that would take them to the tenth floor.

Early the next morning, the site labor foreman took two men to clear the debris piling up in the elevator pit. To his horror, when he reached his destination, he saw Bob's limp body lying amongst the rubbish, with his skull caved in, evidently the result of a fall from high above.

The subsequent investigation quickly turned into a bizarre affair, for when the police visited the elevator company, they discovered that the business card given to Bob Lane was a forgery, and the real person by that name was away on vacation. Furthermore, they had not had a visitor from their Italian subsidiary for over six months.

Eyewitnesses at the project site were limited to Bob Lane's assistant and the hoist operator. Still, both could not provide any helpful information, saying only that the visitors were dressed in business attire and one spoke with a foreign accent.

Subsequent investigations led the police up a series of blind allies. And while, technically, the case was still open, unless further information was forthcoming, it looked very much like it would remain an unsolved mystery.

Paul Jeffries attended the lower sixth form at Trinity High, having passed four O-level exams the previous year. During the summer recess, however, his cousin purchased a secondhand car that needed extensive repairs and maintenance, something he asked Paul to help him with. Initially, Paul only agreed to assist as a friendly gesture to a family member he'd always been close with. He became completely enamored with the work within days of starting the project. Previously, he had plans to study electrical engineering, but before the Christmas break arrived, he knew he only wanted to be a mechanic. Realizing that A levels would be of little or no benefit to the career he sought, he left at the end of the school year, having secured an apprenticeship with a local garage.

Paul learned his trade quickly, and while he was required to complete five years of training, his skills were on a par with qualified mechanics by the time he'd turned nineteen.

Upon completing his apprenticeship, Paul received a significant wage increase, and several months later, he could afford a down payment on a secondhand Triumph Spitfire, which soon became the love of his life, that is, until he met Mary.

Following two years of courtship, Paul married his sweetheart in a ceremony held at St. Luke's church, with Bob Lane acting as his best man.

On returning from a honeymoon in Scotland, the newlyweds moved into the spare bedroom at Mary's parent's house, where they saved every penny possible. When their bank account balance reached the amount necessary to secure a mortgage, they purchased a small, semi-detached house in the nearby town of Ware.

Shortly after moving into their new home, Mary fell pregnant, and the following year, she gave birth to a baby boy. Two years later, the family was rounded out with the arrival of a baby girl.

Life for Paul met his expectations, as he continued to receive great satisfaction from his work and enjoyed spending most of his free time with his family. While providing for a wife and two growing kids was occasionally a struggle, Paul wasn't one to place much importance on material possessions. Additionally, as he could maintain and repair items around the house, his family could cut down on those expenses.

One Thursday evening, Mary told her husband that her car had been making some loud and odd noises. This did not surprise Paul, as Mary's Morris Minor was well past its prime. The owner of the garage where Paul worked allowed his mechanics free access on Sundays if they wanted to use the facility for personal repair work. Consequently, Paul promised his wife he'd take care of her car the following weekend.

The weather forecast indicated Sunday would be warm and sunny, so Mary asked Paul if they could take a day trip to Woburn Abbey. Knowing his family would want to leave home by mid-morning, Bob rose at six o'clock to have enough time to fix his wife's car before taking off on their outing.

Arriving at the garage shortly after sunrise, Bob unlocked the workshop door and drove his wife's car into the bay designated for his use. He jacked up the vehicle to a height that would allow him to inspect the undercarriage and removed the two front wheels that appeared to be a part of the problem. When he finished diagnosing the problems, he collected the tools necessary for the repairs.

Mary got out of bed shortly after Bob left, as she wanted to pack a lunch for their outing and to ensure she and the kids were dressed and ready when Bob arrived home.

Though she'd expected her husband to return around nine o'clock, Mary wasn't overly concerned when he hadn't shown up by half past nine, as she knew some jobs took longer than anticipated. But she became uneasy when the clock struck ten, and Bob had still not returned.

Not wanting to worry the children, Mary told them she had to pop out for some shopping, but she'd be back in less than one hour. This would allow her to drive to the garage in Bob's car to ensure he was okay.

When Mary opened the door to the workshop, she called out Bob's name, as she didn't want to startle him. Absent a response, Mary assumed Bob was in the middle of something whereby he didn't want to be disturbed, so she walked quietly across to the bay where he worked. But to her horror, when she arrived, she saw the front end of her car resting on top of Bob's lifeless body.

The subsequent police investigation proved inconclusive. While it was determined to be extremely unlikely, car jacks would fail, especially when assembled by a professional. There was no evidence to support any other explanation.

Interviews with people in the neighborhood produced nothing of substance. One elderly man said that when looking out from his kitchen window earlier in the morning, he'd seen a car pull up at the workshop, and two men got out and walked toward the workshop door. But as he could not provide any information on the car model or license plate, or any meaningful description of the two men in it, that line of investigation quickly came to a dead end.

There was one student from the class of '62 who had confirmed her attendance at the twenty-five-year reunion but became a no-show without providing prior notice or subsequent explanation.

Diane Coleman was the only child of Ronald (Ronnie) and Sheila Coleman. Ronnie worked as a bookkeeper, and his wife worked part-time at the local library.

Though Diane displayed an inquisitive nature from an early age, she was always reserved, often to the point of appearing to be unsociable. But behind this dour personality lay an intelligent, caring young woman with a sharp wit, albeit one that was sparingly used.

An outstanding student, Diane passed with high grades in all the eight O-level exams she sat for, leaving her class teacher certain that Diane would undoubtedly end up at a prestigious university. But Diane had other ideas. To the surprise of both her parents and her teacher, Diane left school after the fifth form to take up an administrative position in the local library while also enrolling in evening classes to hone her typing skills.

Diane's parents were disappointed by their daughter's decisions, as they believed she had the talent to succeed either as a teacher or in the medical field. They were also concerned that Diane spent most of her evenings alone in her bedroom, rarely socializing or pursuing recreational activities. But despite her parents' disapproval, Diane continued her quest, which was revealed two years later when she disclosed that she'd written a novel. Though her initial attempts to find a publisher had not yet borne fruit, she was encouraged by several of the reviews she received.

Diane spent the next five years writing a variety of books. Though she had a never-quit personality, she began to wonder if writing would always be just a hobby—until the day a letter from a publishing firm arrived. After reluctantly agreeing to several adjustments, Diane's first book was published later that year.

While sales of Diane's work began slowly, they increased with every book she published. By age twenty-seven, she was receiving substantial income from royalties, and by the age of thirty, she'd become a recognized name in her genre.

When Diane turned thirty-five, her father unexpectedly died from a heart attack. This profoundly impacted her mother, who quickly sank into a dark depression. And regrettably, the following year, she also passed away.

Diane's losses made her think carefully about her future and what she wanted from her life. While she continued writing, she started spending more time pursuing charitable activities and travelling to places of interest. While Diane had always been open to marriage, she knew that it would only work for her if she met a man who shared her values, something she felt was increasingly unlikely to happen as time passed.

Finally, coming to terms with the fact that writing and charitable work would be her lot in life, Diane settled into a predictable though largely satisfying routine. Unaccustomed to having surprises, Diane was speechless after receiving a phone call from an acquaintance of years past. While she seldom did anything spontaneously, she even amazed herself when she made a life-changing decision within minutes of putting down the receiver.

Without hesitation, she sold her house and other tangible assets before taking a one-way flight to Rio de Janeiro. Information she only shared with her solicitor.

Sam was extremely grateful to receive Sarah's report, which helped her finally get beyond the guilt that had haunted her since hearing about the tragedies suffered by past students. Nevertheless, she decided to resign from her job at Trinity High. The following year, she took up a new role with a charitable organization, mentoring children with learning disabilities.

THE END

One Dark Night

I'd never enjoyed driving along the Pacific Coast Highway after dark but dealing with the additional challenges of torrential rain and gusty winds really tried my patience. Few things could have made me embark on such a journey, especially late on a stormy winter afternoon, but the phone call I'd received earlier in the day was one of them. I'd long since learned that saying no to Mr. Chow's demands, irrespective of their reasonableness, could be quite detrimental to my livelihood.

Following the call from Mr. Chow's office, I assembled the documents I needed and made a reservation at the inn where I'd be meeting Mr. Chow's representative the following morning, and prior to departing, I phoned my wife to inform her I wouldn't be home until the next day. When she didn't answer, I left a message while making a mental note to call again later. I wasn't away from home often, but on such occasions, I always kept her fully informed. "No exceptions" was the non-negotiable rule. And like most husbands, I knew the likely consequences if I failed to comply!

After driving for what seemed like an eternity with the rain bouncing off my windshield, I saw a sign indicating my destination could be reached by taking the next left turn, then driving for another ten miles. The turnoff led me down a narrow, dark, bumpy road that was practically deserted. Consequently, I was much relieved when a faintly lit sign reading "Sunset Inn" came into view.

The rain hadn't let up, and though I could park my car in the front lot, I was soaked to the skin by the time I reached the entrance door. In the process of checking in, I discovered the restaurant was taking last orders in thirty minutes, so I hurried to my room, where I changed into dry clothes.

Following my getting seated in the dining room, I was in the process of ordering fillet steak and a glass of pinot noir when my mobile phone rang. The unidentified voice said, "When you finish your meal, go immediately to the reception area. A message will be waiting there for you." Then the line went dead.

As the anonymous caller's words echoed back through my mind, I felt myself shudder. *How did they know I was in the dining room? Was someone watching me?* As these thoughts repeated themselves, it dawned on me that the slow mumbling voice I'd just listened to was eerily similar to the one that had spoken to me earlier that morning from Mr. Chow's office.

When my steak finally arrived, I realized that I'd been staring vacantly into space since receiving the disconcerting phone call. In an instant, my appetite disappeared, though I managed to swallow the wine in one gulp. Feeling a need to ease my increasing anxiety, I immediately ordered another glass.

Slowly, my mind turned to the deal I'd done with Mr. Chow several weeks earlier. Admittedly, not everything had gone exactly to plan, but after explaining the circumstances, I'd assumed the matter had been put to rest. Had I underestimated the possible ongoing problems it may have caused? I didn't think so, but I couldn't be sure.

Suddenly, I remembered the rumors I'd heard at the club, where, apparently, mysterious accidents had happened to certain individuals who Mr. Chow felt had let him down. Though, of course, these may have been nothing more than idle gossip.

I sipped my wine and attempted to swallow a small piece of steak. My head was swirling. Should I call the police? A bit drastic, I supposed, and in any event, what would I tell them? Perhaps I should leave and go home. If this was to be my course of action, I should stop drinking immediately. But in a moment of indecision, I found myself ordering yet another refill.

One more mouthful of steak and finishing my third glass of wine did allow me to relax a little. I reminded myself that I hadn't done anything wrong, or at least not intentionally. And if Mr. Chow was truly unhappy with me, surely he wouldn't be proposing another deal. So why on earth was I worrying?

Having convinced myself that I was most likely getting upset about nothing, I signed my meal check and proceeded to the reception area, where I introduced myself to the attendant. Without saying a word, she opened a drawer and handed over a sealed envelope, which I decided to open in the comfort of the cocktail lounge. Though in truth, the real comfort I sought was a large scotch.

After signing a tab for a double Johnnie Walker Blue Label, I chose to sit at an empty table that provided a clear view of the entire bar. As discreetly as possible, I scanned the few customers present before concluding that none of them were paying me any attention. Feeling a little more relaxed, I opened the envelope to find a note typed on a sheet of white paper that read: "Proceed to the public guest phone and dial room number 86."

Again, I carefully checked the occupants in the bar while being careful to avoid eye contact. They all appeared to be actively engaged in conversation, so if one of them was spying on me, they were doing a damn good job of disguising it. Upon weighing up my options, I finished my drink before going to the phone booth, where I dialed room number 86. When the ring tone stopped, the line went silent for several seconds—then a voice said, "Come up to room 86. It's on the third floor. The door is unlocked, so go inside and sit in the armchair beside the bed. Then you will receive further instructions. And don't bring anything or anyone with you." It was the same slow mumbling voice that I'd heard earlier, only now it really gave me the willies!

Following the brief message, the line went dead, and I found myself visibly shaking. *Should I rethink my plan and head home as quickly as possible?* I wondered. Why was I being treated in such a bizarre manner? Surely, it could only be an attempt to intimidate me. But to what end?

I braced myself while trying hard to apply logic to my increasingly jumbled thoughts. If someone was going to injure me, physically or otherwise, running away at this juncture probably wouldn't prevent that from happening. I again reminded myself that I'd done nothing wrong, and because of that, I should have nothing to fear.

I decided it best to proceed as directed, so without further hesitation, I took the elevator to the third floor. There, I strolled down the corridor as casually as my body would allow until I reached room number 86. I stopped momentarily and took a deep breath before opening the door. Only the nightlight was on, but it provided sufficient illumination to see the general layout and contents of what was clearly a very large and luxurious suite. As instructed, I sat in the armchair and waited with all my senses on high alert.

I'd been sitting for about two minutes when suddenly the nightlight went off, and seconds later, the bathroom door opened. Peering through the doorway, I saw two candles burning, which enabled me to see the silhouette of a human being standing between them. The figure stood motionless for a moment before taking a step forward and uttering the words, "So, you've arrived at long last. You must know there's a price to pay for what you've done." It was that same slow mumbling voice that, by now, I found quite terrifying.

The figure took another step in my direction, and though the darkness hid its features, I could see it was holding something in its right hand. I quickly reasoned that it could only be a gun, and while I involuntarily attempted to say the words "Holy fuck!" no sound was forthcoming. Good Lord above, I was only thirty-five years old, but I now knew my life would shortly be coming to an abrupt and premature end!

Frozen with fear, I stared helplessly as the figure slowly edged towards me and lifted both of its arms.

As I awaited my fate, I heard an explosion that echoed around the entire room. Somebody once told me that a fatal bullet rarely causes pain, and one's senses largely remain intact until one finally loses consciousness. As I waited for this to happen, the lights suddenly came on. "Don't be such a coward. Admit that you screwed up!" said the figure, who was now staring me in the face. Speechless as the result of blind fear, I suddenly realized that standing in front of me was my wife, holding a bottle of the champagne she always drank on her birthday in one hand and a corkscrew in the other.

Terry Bush
September 2020

About the Author

Terry Bush was born in London, England. He attended the St Albans College of Building before embarking on a 40+ year career in construction management. During that time, he worked on projects in 11 countries worldwide. In the second half of his career, he co-founded and served as CEO of two construction management companies. He makes his home in Clayton, California.

Made in the USA
Monee, IL
29 July 2023

40054043R00089